Washington
State Facts

Nickname:	The Evergreen State
Date Entered Union:	November 11, 1889 (the 42nd state)
Motto:	*Alki* (By and by)
Washington Men:	Bob Barker, *TV host* Bing Crosby, *singer, actor* Bill Gates, *software executive* Jimi Hendrix, *guitarist* Kenny Loggins, *singer*
Flower:	Pink rhododendron
Song:	"Washington, My Home," words and music by Helen Davis
Fun Facts:	The world's first soft-serve ice cream machine was located in an Olympia Dairy Queen. Starbucks, the biggest coffee chain in the world, was founded in Seattle.

He could have driven home blindfolded

The two-lane road twisted like a snarled fishing line, unreeling through the sawtooth-forested mountain in sharp zigzags. The low-slung Ferrari, not built for back-country roads, thumped roughly over the scarred pavement. Unfazed by the danger, Caine coaxed the car around the deadly narrow switchbacks.

Bruce Spingsteen's "No Surrender" blared from the speakers. Caine punched a button to zap through the song. He damn well wasn't in any mood to reminisce about lost loves.

When he reached one of the few straight stretches on the highway, Caine floored the accelerator: straddling the white centerline, the car streaked toward an enormous truck. The strident warning of the air horn shattered the mountain stillness. Once. Twice. A third time.

Caine refused to budge. He remained as cool as if he were out for a leisurely Sunday afternoon drive instead of barreling hell-bent-for-leather straight toward death.

No retreat. No surrender.

American HEROES
AGAINST ALL ODDS

JoAnn ROSS

The Return of Caine O'Halloran

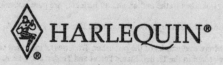

HARLEQUIN®

TORONTO • NEW YORK • LONDON
AMSTERDAM • PARIS • SYDNEY • HAMBURG
STOCKHOLM • ATHENS • TOKYO • MILAN • MADRID
PRAGUE • WARSAW • BUDAPEST • AUCKLAND

To Jay, who refused to give up on us

HARLEQUIN BOOKS
225 Duncan Mill Road, Don Mills,
Ontario, Canada M3B 3K9

ISBN 0-373-82245-6

THE RETURN OF CAINE O'HALLORAN

Copyright © 1994 by JoAnn Ross

This edition published by arrangement with Harlequin Books S.A.

® and TM are trademarks of the publisher. Trademarks indicated with ® are registered in the United States Patent and Trademark Office, the Canadian Trade Marks Office and in other countries.

Visit us at www.eHarlequin.com

Printed in U.S.A.

About the Author

USA Today bestselling romance author **JoAnn Ross** has written over seventy novels and has been published in twenty-six countries, including Russia, China, France and Turkey. Two of her titles have been excerpted in *Cosmopolitan* magazine, and her books have also been published by Doubleday Book Club and the Literary Guild. She's received numerous awards, including a Lifetime Career Achievement Award from *Romantic Times Magazine,* and is a popular conference speaker.

JoAnn lives with her husband in Tennessee, where she gains creative inspiration from the view of the misty Great Smoky Mountains out her home office windows.

Books by JoAnn Ross

Harlequin Temptation

Stormy Courtship #42	*Star-Crossed Lovers* #432
Love Thy Neighbor #67	*Moonstruck Lovers* #436
Duskfire #77	*The Prince & the Showgirl* #453
Without Precedent #96	*Lovestorm* #471
A Hero at Heart #115	*Angel of Desire* #482
Magic in the Night #126	*The Return of Caine O'Halloran* #489
Playing for Keeps #137	*Scandals* #406
Tempting Fate #153	*Never a Bride* #537
Hot on the Trail #171	*For Richer or Poorer* #541
Worth Waiting For #187	*Three Grooms and a Wedding* #545
Spirit of Love #193	*Private Passions* #562
In a Class by Himself #201	*The Outlaw* #585
Wilde 'N Wonderful #209	*Untamed* #605
Eve's Choice #221	*Wanted!* #609
Murphy's Law #233	*Ambushed* #613
Guarded Moments #296	*Roarke: The Adventurer* #638
Tangled Hearts #333	*Shayne: The Pretender* #646
Tangled Lives #345	*Michael: The Defender* #654
Dark Desires #382	*Hunk of the Month* #683
The Knight in Shining Armor #409	*1-800-Hero* #693
	Mackenzie's Woman #717

* * * * * *

Harlequin Love & Laughter	Harlequin Intrigue
I Do, I Do...For Now	*Risky Pleasure* #27
	Bait and Switch #36
Yours Truly	
It Happened One Week	

Dear Reader,

I've always enjoyed writing stories about reunited lovers. Those of you who read my 1992 Valentine's story, *A Very Special Delivery,* might remember that I married my first love. What I didn't mention in the letter accompanying the story was that Jay and I were divorced after nine years of marriage. Although the reasons for our breakup were not as tragic as Caine and Nora's, they were painful.

We were apart for two years, during which time we both grew up and changed a great deal. Back then, Jay's career involved a lot of traveling, but he returned to town frequently to visit our son. It was during those visits that we began to realize we each liked the person the other had become. That awareness, coupled with a very strong love that never died, made us decide to try again.

We've never had any reason to regret that decision. In fact, the only problem we had was figuring out how to count the number of years we'd been married. And that little dilemma was solved when Nora Roberts told me that Dear Abby advises remarried couples to include all the years from the beginning of their first marriage. Deciding that few people know more about romance than Nora and Dear Abby, that's what we've done.

In our case, as in Caine and Nora's, love truly is better the second time around.

Happy reading!

JoAnn Ross

Please address questions and book requests to:
Harlequin Reader Service
U.S.: 3010 Walden Ave., P.O. Box 1325, Buffalo, NY 14269
Canadian: P.O. Box 609, Fort Erie, Ont. L2A 5X3

CHAPTER One Chapter

Leon in the glitter, I-I-I three rushing to the sea
the some (-brilly realize now the (mark-larry what
what. The how chord glow by shout made actually
learn Dal row that what and pound ds chrome Sujan
to re/Through the some us crackhill mark it an
lin-rise.
Glory Bowe no sale any-bursus whin work-O
pharmer-nds mill his-rid

_____ **1** _____

HE COULD HAVE DRIVEN home blindfolded.

The two-lane road twisted like a snarled fishing line, unreeling through the sawtooth-forested mountains in sharp zigzags that defied compass reckoning. To make matters worse, the spring thaw had pitted the asphalt, creating a new season of dangerous dips and washouts. The low-slung black Ferrari, not built for back-country roads, thumped roughly over the scarred pavement.

Unfazed by the danger, Caine O'Halloran coaxed the hell-on-wheels beast around the deadly narrow switchbacks with the same practiced skill and clever touch he'd used to coax last night's redhead to climax.

The engine behind his head whined as the revs rose and fell; blaring from the four amplified stereo speakers, Bruce Springsteen was advising "no surrender." Caine's fingers tapped out the driving rhythm of drums and acoustic guitar on the top of the steering wheel. Towering trees—Pacific silver fir, Western hemlock and the majestic Douglas fir—screened both sides of the roadway, making it seem as if he were racing through a narrow green alley.

Those same trees were reflected in the lenses of Caine's dark glasses. Although the sky overhead was the hue of tarnished silver, a few sunbeams managed to slant through the curtain of trees, laying shimmering stripes of light across the pavement.

The sound of moving water was everywhere as streams

born in melting glaciers fed the rivers running to the sea. The scent of freshly cut fir rode the brisk spring wind.

When The Boss started singing about missing Bobby Jean, Caine leaned forward and punched a chrome button to zip through the song. He damn well wasn't in any mood to reminisce about lost loves.

"'Glory Days'," he said approvingly when the CD player stopped on the familiar lyrics.

One night a few years ago, after he'd played it three times on the jukebox in a Minneapolis bar, a winsome coed from the University of Minnesota had informed him that it was really a song about faded dreams and lost opportunities.

Caine hadn't believed that then, and he sure as hell didn't now. To him it would always be The Boss's tribute to athletes who possessed blazing speedballs that made other guys look like fools. Guys like Caine O'Halloran.

He sped past a runaway-truck escape ramp that looked like a ski jump, downshifted as he approached yet another twist in the road, then punched the gas pedal. The Ferrari rocketed out of the turn like a moon shot.

Cornering in a Ferrari wasn't for the faint of heart. The speedometer shot upward and the tachometer approached the red line as the speed of the Testarossa blurred the trees. The force of three hundred and eighty horses fully opened up pushed him back against the onyx leather seats. The engine's shriek rivaled that of a fighter jet.

When he reached one of the few straight stretches on the highway, Caine floored the accelerator; straddling the white centerline, the car streaked toward an enormous truck loaded with logs.

The Peterbilt log truck was the same green as the fir trees flashing by the Ferrari's tinted windows. Tall chrome stacks emitted billowy puffs of diesel exhaust, like smoke signals.

The strident warning of the air horn shattered the mountain stillness.

Once.

Twice.

A third time.

Smiling with grim determination, Caine refused to budge. The asphalt stretched between car and truck like a shiny black ribbon. All the time he remained as cool as if he were out for a leisurely Sunday-afternoon drive in the country, instead of barreling hell-bent-for-leather straight to his death. *No retreat; no surrender.* The rock refrain pounded in his head; adrenaline raced through his blood like a drug.

The air horn, now a steady, impatient bleat, split the air.

Time took on the strange feel of an instant slow-motion replay as Caine became vividly aware of the staccato flash of white lines disappearing beneath the Ferrari's wide radial tires, of the sun glancing off the chrome stack of the truck, of the driver's red-and-black plaid shirt, of his orange-billed cap, of his grizzled gray beard and finally, as the truck came even closer, of the man's expression: first disbelief, then fright, finally fury.

No retreat. No surrender.

Caine waited fatalistically for the bearded man to make his move.

At the last possible second, the truck veered; its right wheels went off the road, scattering gravel. Caine got a fleeting glimpse of a stocky, raised middle finger.

A moment later, a Bronco that had been following the Peterbilt passed Caine, as well. The driver stared at the Ferrari in obvious disbelief.

Caine watched the trucks disappear in his rearview mirror. When he'd been seventeen, speeding around these hairpin curves in a fire-engine-red Trans Am convertible, emerging victorious from a game of chicken with the ubiquitous log trucks had always left him feeling vividly alive.

But after today's near-death encounter, he felt strangely let down. And disappointed. As Springsteen's gravelly voice began singing about "working on the highway," a hangover Caine had nearly forgotten after crossing the Oregon-Washington State border and entering the Olympic Peninsula came crashing back.

THE NEWS SPREAD THROUGH the town of Tribulation like wildfire. Caine O'Halloran was back.

Dr. Nora Anderson was on duty in her clinic when she received the unexpected bulletin from her eight-year-old nephew who'd become airborne after turning a corner too fast on his Bart Simpson skateboard. The landing, not soft, had been on a gravel driveway.

"Did you hear the neat-o news?" Eric Anderson asked, trying with youthful bravado not to flinch as Nora picked pieces of cinder from his palm with a pair of surgical tweezers.

"Eric," his mother chided, "your aunt is trying to concentrate."

Karin Anderson's voice was edged with a stern warning tone that made Nora look up. "What news?"

"Caine got cut from the Yankees," Eric told her. "But Jimmy Olson told me that his dad told him that Caine was comin' home to live here while he gets his arm back in shape.

"We saw his car parked outside The Log Cabin," he

said. "You should see it, Aunt Nora! It looks just like the Batmobile!"

A ratmobile was more like it. And to be hanging around a bar in the middle of the afternoon! Obviously, Caine hadn't changed. "It's true," Karin said, her blue eyes offering sympathy.

"Well, I hope things work out for him," Nora said calmly. She'd sealed any feelings concerning Caine O'Halloran inside her, years ago. It was easier. Safer.

"Do you think he'll give me a ride in his car, huh, Aunt Nora?" Eric asked hopefully. "After all, we are kinda related."

Nora knew that Eric used his aunt's former marriage to the baseball star to gain points on the playground. Understanding a small boy's obsession with heroes—even ones undeserving of such loyalty—Eric's behavior had never bothered her.

But then again, Caine hadn't been living in Tribulation, either.

"I don't know," she answered. Never having been able to predict her ex-husband's behavior, she certainly wasn't going to start trying to guess what was going through his adolescent mind now. "You'll have to ask him that yourself." She tackled another piece of gravel.

"Ouch!" Eric yanked his hand back.

"Sorry." She'd used more force than necessary. Damn Caine, anyway.

Although she'd been in her first year of medical school during their brief and stormy marriage, he hadn't believed her when she'd insisted that she didn't intend to let marriage or motherhood interfere with her plans to be a doctor.

No, Nora corrected now. It wasn't that Caine hadn't believed her; it was more that he hadn't listened. By the time she'd been married a week, Nora had realized that her husband possessed the unique ability to hear only what he wanted to hear.

"Well, I think that's all of it," she said, giving her nephew's hand one last antiseptic wash. Nora turned to her sister-in-law. "If I were you, I'd hide that skateboard."

"I'm turning it into kindling the minute we get home."

"Mom!" Color returned to Eric's cheeks, staining them as red as the raspberries that grew wild in the forest surrounding the mountain town.

"We'll discuss this later," Karin said firmly. "At home. With your father."

His shoulders slumped disconsolately. "Dad'll side with you. He always does."

Although she agreed with Karin's decision to deny Eric further skateboard privileges, Nora's heart went out to her nephew. "Hey, Eric..."

His bottom lip was thrust out over his top one. "What?"

She tossed him a couple of the silver dollars Karl Mahlstrom had paid his bill with earlier that morning. The retired mill worker had returned from Reno, Nevada, with paper cups filled with coins and a stiff shoulder from eighteen hours at the slot machines.

"Why don't you take your mom out for some ice cream?"

The pout wavered, a reluctant smile played at the corners of his lips. "Okay," he agreed with an outward lack of enthusiasm that Nora knew was mostly feigned. Then, remembering his manners, he said, "Thanks, Aunt Nora."

"You're welcome." Nora exchanged another long look with her sister-in-law. *We'll talk about Caine later*, Karin's look said.

Not on a bet, Nora's answered.

It was Monday, the day of the week when a steady

stream of patients always showed up at the clinic, showing the effects of a weekend of recreational abuse.

On top of that, her nurse, Kirstin Lundstrom, was still on maternity leave. Nora had to serve as nurse, doctor and office clerk, which meant that she barely had time to catch her breath all day.

Not that Nora minded the hectic pace; she was grateful that she didn't have time to think about Caine O'Halloran's return. And what, if anything, that would mean to her life.

Returning to Washington's Olympic Peninsula to practice family medicine in her hometown of two hundred and fifty residents meant that Nora saw her patients at the grocery store, or weeding their flower gardens, or over potato salad at a church potluck social.

It also meant that she was more likely to be intimately involved with a patient, so that a serious illness or a death touched her more than it had at the big-city hospitals where she'd worked before returning home to Tribulation.

Many of her patients had lost their health insurance, along with their jobs. They were people too poor to pay for visits to the doctor, but too proud to ask for government assistance. Although the condition of the Northwest's logging and fishing industries had not been struck a fatal blow, recovery was a long time coming to this isolated forest community. In order to finance her new clinic, which she'd set up in the hundred-year-old house she'd inherited from her grandmother, Nora also made the thirty-five-mile round trip to Port Angeles to work in the hospital emergency room.

Her clinic was open on Monday, Wednesday and Friday; she worked at the emergency room on Tuesdays, Thursdays and Saturdays. Although sleep was as rare as it had been during the grueling thirty-six-hour shifts of her internship, not once had she regretted her decision.

Her work in the emergency room, while fulfilling in its own way, paid the bills and put food on the table. Her work at the clinic—caring for family, friends and neighbors—fed her soul.

The complaints today were relatively minor and she wasn't surprised that every one of her patients wanted to talk about Caine's return to Tribulation.

"Caine'll be back on the mound by the All-Star break," Johnny Duggan informed her after she'd given him a sample package of antihistamine to soothe some yellowjacket stings that hadn't responded to calamine lotion. "That boy always was a pistol."

Since Johnny was Caine's third cousin on his mother's side, Nora could understand the man's loyalty.

The next member of the Caine O'Halloran fan club was Ingrid Johansson, who'd run the Timberline Café since long before Nora was born. The elderly woman had strained a back muscle getting a box of steak sauce down from a too-high shelf.

"If the boy could come back from that torn rotor cuff three years ago, this new injury won't be any problem," Ingrid predicted as she paid her bill. The worn, rumpled dollar bills, smelling faintly of chain-saw gasoline, were evidence of a clientele consisting mainly of loggers.

"Oh, I brought you something," Ingrid said. "For giving my Lars that cough medicine last week for no charge."

She handed Nora a brown paper bag from which rose an enticing scent of warm apples and brown sugar. "It's a strudel," she added unnecessarily.

"Thanks." Nora could envision the cellulite leaping to her thighs from the aroma alone. "It smells delicious."

She'd already gained ten pounds since returning to Tribulation, mostly from her patients' peach cobblers, berry pies, fresh-caught—and thankfully cleaned—fish, corn muffins and numerous other local delicacies.

It was as if everyone realized she was undercharging them for their visits, and although they were grateful, pride insisted that they augment the reduced fee with whatever they could spare.

"I figured you could use a little fattening up." Ingrid's bright eyes swept judiciously over Nora's slender frame. "You're not gonna get yourself a man unless you put a little more meat on those bones."

"Actually, I've been too busy to even think about men."

"Well, I expect that'll change, now that Caine's back in town," the older woman declared.

"My marriage to Caine ended a long time ago," Nora replied, reluctant to be discussing something so personal, but feeling that her disinterest in Caine O'Halloran needed to be put on record.

And who better to start with than Ingrid? Nora doubted that there was a person in Tribulation who didn't pop into the eatery sometime during the week. Especially on Wednesdays, for Ingrid's pot-roast special.

"Legally," Ingrid agreed, closing her pocketbook with a snap. "My experience has been that feelings are quite another kettle of fish."

Determined to get the last word in, she left the office without giving Nora an opportunity to respond.

For the rest of the day, Nora continued to smile and nod and write prescriptions and listen to yet another story depicting the life and times of Tribulation's local hero.

Twenty-one years ago, Tribulation, a timber town founded a century earlier by a Swedish logger and an

Irishman who'd been laying railroad tracks up the coast, had gone through hard times.

People who could trace their roots back to those original settlers had been forced to leave their homes and seek what they hoped would be temporary employment in the Puget Sound cities of Seattle, Olympia and Tacoma.

Storefronts had been boarded up; the school established by the founding fathers had been in danger of closing, which would have forced the students to be bused to Port Angeles. Morale had been at an all-time low.

Until a cocky fourteen-year-old took the pitcher's mound during a state high school championship game between the Tribulation Loggers and the Richland Bombers and threw what Washington sportswriters the next morning were calling "the pitch heard 'round the state."

From that day on, Caine O'Halloran was known as The Golden Boy with the Golden Arm. His natural ability to throw a ball gained him fame and admirers and his hometown was eager to bask in the reflected glow of his popularity.

He went to college on an athletic scholarship, then on to play professional baseball. He spent some time in the minors because although his fastball flew at ballistic speed, no one, including Caine, ever had any idea exactly where it was going.

A sportswriter for the *Seattle Journal* once remarked that O'Halloran, then playing for the Tacoma Athletics, didn't throw to spots, he threw to continents.

However, with time, he'd garnered control and began making headlines for his energetic play both on and off the baseball diamond as he moved from team to team, league to league, barreling into every new town like a hired gun, paid to win championships. Which he did, with almost monotonous regularity.

He was one of those rare, powerful athletes known as a "closer"—a pitcher brought to the mound in the last innings to win the game. And like so many relief pitchers Nora had met during her brief marriage, Caine was a bit mad. Mad angry, and mad crazy.

One particular stunt she recalled vividly was during his stint at Tacoma when he'd relieved the boredom of waiting to be called to the mound by telephoning other bullpens throughout the Pacific Coast League. By imitating the voices of the other teams' coaches, he'd ordered relievers hundreds of miles away to begin warming up.

The prank had resulted in a hundred-dollar fine and more nationwide publicity than money ever could have purchased.

But now, according to the articles she'd read, Caine's golden arm had turned to brass and his most recent team, the New York Yankees, had put him on waivers.

Speculation ran rampant concerning his future; doctors who'd never examined him were interviewed on television and in the papers, their prognoses ranging from Caine's return in time for the fall playoffs, to the prediction that his career was over. The one thing every article agreed upon was that Caine refused to accept that his playing days were over.

Which wasn't surprising, since in Nora's experience, most athletes possessed a seemingly genetic inability to accept the fact that their bodies might be more fragile than their determination. Or their egos.

The afternoon was almost over when Karl Larstrom, a rough-hewn former logger in his late seventies, showed up at the clinic without an appointment, his seven-year-old great-grandson in tow.

"Gunnar here got a fishhook in his ear," he advised her

laconically. "Tried to clip it off with a pair of wire cutters, but it won't budge."

Nora smiled down at the boy whose wet blue eyes suggested he'd been crying. "Hi, Gunnar," she greeted him. "Why don't you hop up here and I'll see what we can do."

"I've been teaching the boy how to cast," Karl told her while she worked on the metal fishhook firmly imbedded in the boy's earlobe. "Guess he needs a mite more practice."

"It was the damn tree," Gunnar insisted, flinching when Nora experimentally jiggled the hook. "It got in the way."

"Watch your mouth, boy," Karl advised. "Your mama's not gonna let you keep fishing with me if she thinks I'm teaching you how to cuss."

"But that's what you said when the line got tangled in the first place," Gunnar argued. "Ow!"

"Those trees are infamous for eating fishing lines," Nora assured the boy, who'd gone pale.

"I suspect you heard about Caine," Karl Larstrom offered.

A spot of bright red blood beaded where the now freed hook had entered the skin. Nora swabbed at the minuscule hole with alcohol.

"Several times. All done," she declared, hoping to forestall any more conversation concerning Caine.

"Joe Bob Carroll saw him driving toward town around noon."

"Really?" Nora asked in a tone of absolute disinterest.

"Yup." Karl had never been one to pick up on subtlety. "He was driving one of them fancy Eye-talian sports cars." He reached into his pocket and pulled out some bills.

"So Eric told me." Nora put the rumpled money in the

cashbox she kept in the top drawer. Instead of gasoline, these dollar bills smelled vaguely of fish. "He said it looked like a Batmobile."

"Yup," Karl said after chewing the description over for a moment. "I reckon it does, at that. Did Eric tell you about him playing chicken with Harmon Olson's log truck?"

Despite her determination to ignore every bit of unwelcome news about her former husband, that particular tidbit earned her reluctant attention.

"He wasn't!"

"Joe Bob Carroll was right behind Harmon's Peterbilt in his Bronco." Karl's eyes brightened when he realized he'd finally hit on a piece of information Nora hadn't already heard.

"I thought you and Gunnar were out fishing all day."

"We were. But word gets around."

"Tell me about it," she murmured.

Gossip is the motherlode of small towns and in this case, Tribulation's grapevine was obviously working at warp speed.

"Caine was riding the centerline, just the way he did back when he was workin' overtime to be the town hellion, and from the way Joe Bob tells it, it looked like he wasn't gonna move, come hell or high water."

Obviously, Caine hadn't changed one little bit. Not that she would have expected him to.

Stupid reckless idiot!

Although she told herself that she didn't care what happened to Caine, Nora had spent too many years in the chaos of emergency rooms, trying to save lives, to stand for anyone foolish enough to risk throwing his life away.

"I take it Harmon gave in."

"Yup. I expect Caine'll drop in at The Log Cabin to have

a drink with his old friends. In case you wanna stop by," he added slyly.

Just what she needed—another matchmaker. Nora quickly declined but after Karl and Gunner had left she couldn't stop her troubled thoughts from drifting to The Log Cabin and to Caine O'Halloran.

2

IF TRIBULATION, Washington, brought to mind the type of neat little New England villages that had proliferated at the turn of the century, it was because the residents preferred to keep it that way. It was a town of Nordic cleanliness, where shop owners still swept the sidewalks each morning and the streets remained as clean as a Swedish kitchen.

A traveler leaving the interstate would find no franchise restaurants in Tribulation; there were more churches—three—than taverns—one—and the movie theater was only open on weekend nights. The crack of Little League bats was heard on Saturday mornings, the chime of church bells on Sundays.

When he'd first arrived in America from his native Sweden, Olaf Anderson, one of the founders of Tribulation, had worked as a lumberjack in the forests of Maine. During those frigid winter months when logging came to a standstill, he would migrate down to Massachusetts, or Vermont, where he worked as a handyman. Eventually, he'd made his way to Washington.

Since he'd thoroughly enjoyed his time in the East, it had seemed a reasonable idea to build a replica of a New England village in this wild Western territory.

Olaf's best friend, Darcy O'Halloran, a wild Irish, harddrinking Saturday-night brawler and jig dancer, had argued that the unruly land cloaked in a tangle of forests, steep mountains and deeply glaciated valleys bore scant resemblance to New England.

But Olaf had a very clear vision of the town he and Darcy would build together. A town that Olaf planned to name New Stockholm, while Darcy held out for New Dublin.

For a time it seemed the settlement of loggers, miners and fishermen would go nameless. Finally, after they'd been arguing for nearly a year, one frustrated citizen suggested they call the town Tribulation. The moniker, Olaf and Darcy decided, fitted nicely in a region that already boasted a Mount Despair, Mount Triumph, Torment, Forbidden, and Paradise.

More than a century later, the centerpiece of Tribulation remained a wide, grassy, green square. A fountain bubbled at one end of the green, a horseshoe pit was at the other. A clock tower, made of dark red brick that had weathered to a dusky pink over the century, could be spotted for miles in all directions.

In the middle of the green square was a lacy white Victorian bandstand, erected in the early 1900s by an O'Halloran ancestor who'd believed that every town needed a band. Beside the bandstand was a larger-than-life-size wooden statue of Olaf Anderson, erected by one of his descendants in the 1940s. A woodpecker, displaying uncanny precision, had pecked a hole in the statue's posterior.

Across from the square, between the post office and the fire station, was the gray-stone three-story city hall, the tallest structure, save for the clock tower, in town. The bronze plaque on the cornerstone revealed that the building had been erected in 1899. It also named the mayor of Tribulation at the time, Lars Anderson, and the builder, Donovan O'Halloran.

Although he'd been born into one of the town's founding families, Caine's ambition had always been to get out. Firmly believing that he was meant for life in the fast lane, he'd always found Tribulation's slow pace and old-fashioned, unchanging ways suffocating.

Slate clouds threatened in a darkening gray sky as Caine drove through the two-block downtown area, through a residential neighborhood of neat frame houses trimmed with colorful shutters, then turned onto the graded road out of town.

Drawn by emotions too complex to consider, he stopped the Ferrari in front of the wrought-iron gates of the Pioneer Cemetery, cut the engine and sat there, his hands draped over the steering wheel.

A rush of unbidden, unwanted memories flooded his mind. Memories of a little boy, plump cheeks pink from the brisk spring winds, smiling mouth stained with strawberries, a beloved green-and-yellow Oakland A's cap perched rakishly atop his blond curls, his husky legs pumping away as he ran toward the front door, eager, as always, to go anywhere with his daddy.

Daddy. The word tore at Caine, even now, years later. He pulled a pack of cigarettes from his breast pocket, shook out a cigarette, lighted it with the dashboard lighter, then slumped back into the leather seat and drew the acrid, yet soothing smoke deep into his lungs.

He sure as hell hadn't planned for Nora Anderson to get pregnant. On his way from a farm team in Montana to his new Triple A team in Tacoma, Caine had made the fatal mistake of stopping off in Tribulation the night of the Midsummer Eve festival.

Nora, a senior at the University of Washington at the time, had also been home for the weekend; at first Caine hadn't recognized his best friend's little sister.

The heavy, dark-framed glasses that had always made her look like a studious little owl had been replaced by contacts, the ugly metal braces had come off, leaving behind straight, dazzling-white teeth, and although she could never have been called voluptuous, the skinny angles he'd remembered had been replaced by slender curves in all the right places.

The young woman Nora had become had proved different from the sex-crazed baseball Annies Caine was accustomed to. Not only was she gorgeous in a quiet, understated way, she was also sweet and intelligent. And she'd smelled damn good, too.

Caine had offered to drive Nora home. When he'd taken a detour to his cabin, she hadn't offered a word of complaint.

And when he'd drawn her into his arms, she'd come. Willingly. Eagerly.

When he'd left Tribulation the following morning, Caine hadn't expected to see Nora again. After all, he had his rising career, and she'd soon be off to medical school.

Six weeks later, Caine's mother, of all people, had called him with the unwelcome news.

He'd definitely been less than thrilled when he'd learned he was going to be a father, but baseball players were supposed to at least appear to be wholesome, upstanding role models for America's youth. And as much as he'd hated the idea of giving up his carefree sexual lifestyle, Caine had known that knocking up, and then abandoning some innocent hometown girl just didn't fit the image.

Nora had been no more eager to marry than he was. But after some painfully stilted discussion and not a little coaxing from both families, they'd reluctantly decided that marriage would be in the best interests of their un-

born child. After the baby was born, they would divorce
and go their separate ways.

The kicker had come when Nora had argued against allowing possible emotional entanglements to interfere
with what was nothing more than a legal contrivance.
And although Caine hadn't been wild about the prospect
of celibate cohabitation, he'd agreed to her condition.

So he'd done his duty, albeit grudgingly. And although
he hadn't exactly been husband of the year, neither had he
ever—despite Nora's frequent angry accusations—been
unfaithful.

Then, six months after their shotgun marriage, Dylan
had come crashing into his life, all eight pounds, twelve
ounces of him, and Caine had fallen head over heels in
love.

Exhaling a long, weary breath, Caine leaned his head
back against the car seat, closed his eyes and pressed his
fingers tightly against his lids, trying to block out memories too painful to remember. But the indelible images remained, reaching out across the intervening years.

Sixteen months after Dylan's birth, Caine had been
called up to the majors. He'd packed a case of beer, cold
cuts from the deli and his son into the car and headed off
to his cabin for a poker game with his teammates to celebrate having finally achieved his lifelong dream.

He was going to The Show.

"Hot damn, Dylan," he'd said, buckling the baby into
the padded car seat. "Your daddy's gonna be a big
leaguer! What do you think about that?"

"Bid beader!" Dylan had clapped his hands, picking up
on his father's good mood.

Caine had laughed. God, how he'd loved his son!

Two hours later, Dylan was gone—taken away by a

cruel twist of fate and a drunk driver. In that one fleeting second, Caine's entire life had fallen apart.

And nine years later, he still hadn't figured out how to deal with the loss.

Cursing viciously, Caine crushed his cigarette into the ashtray, then twisted the key in the ignition; tires squealed as he slammed down on the accelerator, ignoring the posted speed limit. He needed a drink, dammit. And he needed it *now*. Less than five minutes later, he pulled the Ferrari into the parking lot of The Log Cabin, spraying gravel in all directions.

Like everything else about Tribulation, The Log Cabin hadn't changed. Oley Severson was still behind the bar, where he'd been for as long as anyone could remember.

Caine stood just inside the doorway for a moment, allowing his eyes to adapt to the lighting that was purposefully dim to keep customers from complaining about smudges on the bar glasses. Not that any of the locals would dare, but there were more and more tourists these days and everyone knew that city folk tended to be finicky.

Neon signs advertising a variety of beers glowed in the smoky haze. Mounted trophy-size steelhead trout and salmon Oley had pulled in from northwestern streams and the Pacific Ocean adorned the knotty-pine walls. Along with the fish were antique signs dating from when Oley's great-grandfather had opened the tavern designed to serve the needs of thirsty timbermen.

One hand-carved wooden sign, hearkening back to the days when a drunken logger could rent a cot in the back room to sleep it off, advised that lumberjacks must remove boots before getting into bed. Another instructed patrons to check their firearms with the bartender.

"Come on in, boy," Oley greeted Caine. "We're all

waiting to hear about your tussle with Harmon Olson's new Peterbilt."

All was certainly the definitive word, Caine decided, glancing around the smoky tavern. Nearly the entire male population of Tribulation was sitting around the scarred wooden tables or perched atop the barstools.

Most of the men were wearing the traditional logger's uniform—plaid, striped or denim shirt; red suspenders; denim pants cut off midcalf to prevent snagging in the underbrush; and leather high-topped, hobnailed calk boots.

Either everyone was out of work or they'd quit early to watch Harmon Olson beat the tar out of him. Entertainment being what it was around these parts, Caine couldn't really blame them.

"News gets around fast," he said, trying not to reveal his concern to learn that it had been Olson's truck he'd been playing chicken with. Every one of the Olson boys was the size of a redwood and their tempers were legendary.

"Joe Bob, here, was followin' Harmon to Forks in his Bronco." Oley nodded toward a redheaded man on a nearby stool as he filled a mug with draft beer. "When he saw you, he hightailed it back here to spread the word."

Despite the pain behind his eyes, Caine managed a lopsided grin for his old high school teammate as he crossed the sawdust-covered floor. Joe Bob Carroll had been his catcher on the Tribulation Loggers.

"I thought you looked familiar." Caine slapped his old friend on the back. "But I was goin' too fast to get a decent look at you."

And if he'd only gotten a better look at Harmon Olson, he'd be out scrounging up a thick piece of timber for self-protection.

"You were movin' like a bat outta hell," Joe Bob said, a

smile splitting his face. "There sure wouldn't've been much left of you or that fancy car, if Harmon hadn't chickened out."

There were eleven rickety stools in front of the L-shaped bar. Ten were occupied; the eleventh, Caine determined, had been saved for him. He climbed up beside Joe Bob and hooked the heels of his cowboy boots over the pine rung encircling the stool.

"But he did chicken out," Caine said.

"Seems he did," Joe Bob agreed. "For now." His tone was that of a man who'd witnessed the lighting of the fuse and was now waiting patiently for the TNT to blow sky-high.

"But I gotta warn you, Caine, Harmon does tend to think right highly of that new truck. I wouldn't want to be the guy who caused it to get all those fresh gravel dings."

There was a murmur of agreement from the other men in the bar, all of whom had had their own hassles with the Olson boys.

"No point in borrowin' trouble." Oley pushed the beer toward Caine. Foam spilled down the side of the mug, puddled on the bar and went ignored. The Log Cabin had never been the type of place to hand out cocktail napkins.

Caine took a long drink of the icy brew, then put the mug down on the bar, making a new ring. He wiped the foam off his mouth with the back of his hand and lit a cigarette.

"Real good to have you back home again," a man next to Joe Bob offered.

"Hiya, Johnny," Caine greeted his cousin. "It's good to be home." He nodded toward Dana Anderson, who'd once been his brother-in-law and had stayed his friend. "Dana."

"Caine. Good to have you back.... Heard the Yankees

cut you," Dana said carefully. They'd drawn straws before Caine had arrived to see who'd broach the sensitive subject, and he had unluckily drawn the short one. "We're all sorry about that."

Caine downed the beer in thirsty swallows and pushed the empty mug toward Oley, who filled it to the brim. Just as he didn't spend money needlessly on cocktail napkins, Oley had never believed in wasting a fresh glass every time a customer wanted a refill. He took Caine's money and put it away in the King Edward cigar box he used as a cash register.

"It's not that big a deal," Caine insisted. "The feeling in my arm is coming back more every day. I figure I'll be back on the mound before the All-Star break."

"For what team?" a man in the back of the bar dared ask.

Caine shot a quick glare through the haze. "Any team that needs a championship," he retorted.

"Well," Tom Anderson, Dana's twin brother, said, "we're all rootin' for you, Caine."

A murmur of agreement went around the room. "So," Joe Bob said, bravely forging his way deeper into dangerous conversational waters, "is it true what the papers are sayin'? That you shocked yourself with an electric drill?"

"Although it's embarrassing as hell, that's what happened," Caine said. "At first I had some weakness in my arm. But I've been working out and the strength's coming back."

He took another drink. Talking about his accident made Caine thirsty. "I'll be back to one hundred percent in no time."

"Is that what the doctors say?" Joe Bob ventured carefully.

Caine frowned down at the white foam topping his

beer. "You know doctors," he said finally. "They won't commit to anything for fear of getting a malpractice suit, I guess. But I know my body better than any damn doctor and I say it's getting better."

He chugged the beer down, seeking alcohol's soothing properties. "Injuries are part of the game," he muttered. "Everyone knows that. The problem is that too many sportswriters and owners and managers—hell, even some fans—all want to be the first to predict the end of a guy's career."

A low murmur of sympathetic agreement circled the room. Caine slammed the mug down on the bar with more force than necessary. "When I retire, it's going to be because I want to. Because playing baseball isn't any fun anymore, or maybe even because I can't win."

His tone implied that he considered that alternative a major impossibility. "And no owner or manager or sportswriter or goddamn quack doctor is going to make that decision for me."

Silence descended.

"Hey, Oley," Caine called out, realizing that he was to blame for the dark mood. "How about a round of drinks to celebrate the prodigal's return?"

For the next few hours, Caine bought beer after beer for his hometown fans and congratulated himself on having the good sense to return to a place where a guy didn't have to throw a four-seam fastball ninety-five miles an hour to prove himself a man.

Much, much later, the door to the bar opened.

Bottles, glasses and mugs were slowly lowered to tables as every man in The Log Cabin stared at Harmon Olson, back from delivering his load of logs. Standing beside him was his brother Kirk.

Looking at Harmon, Caine was sorry to see that his

memory hadn't been playing tricks on him. The elder Olson boy was every bit as big as he'd remembered. And Kirk, unbelievably, was even bigger.

The Olson brothers were forest-hardened males who, like so many of the men in the bar, had come into manhood wrestling with behemoths of timber twenty times their weight. Harmon's torso had thickened with age, but his muscles still bulged like boulders beneath the red-and-black plaid sleeves of his shirt, and his arms were the size of smoked hams.

His hands possessed long thick fingers that could encircle a man's throat with the same deliberate ease they circled an ax handle. Beneath a gray 1950s-style crew cut, Harmon's eyes looked like hard gray stones; his beard resembled steel wool.

His baby brother Kirk's hair was still blond and curly; his face was reddened from working outside. His beefy hands were curled at his sides into enormous loose fists and he looked every bit as dangerous as his Viking ancestors.

"That your damn Ferrari, O'Halloran?" Harmon's rough loud voice reminded Caine of the bugling of a bull elk in mating season.

"Guilty."

Caine pushed off the stool with a sigh. He'd always considered himself a lover, not a fighter, and he usually managed to talk his way out of altercations. Unfortunately, neither Harmon nor Kirk looked as if they'd dropped into The Log Cabin for afternoon conversation.

"You near caused me to roll my new truck," Harmon growled. He began rolling up his sleeves, revealing rock-hard forearms. A bluish purple tattoo had been etched into the dark flesh below his right elbow; of what, Caine couldn't quite tell.

"You know, I'm really sorry about that, Harmon," Caine said with an ingratiating smile.

The Olson brothers walked toward him, mayhem on their minds and faces. Behind him, Caine heard chair legs scraping against the sawdust-covered floor as onlookers hurried to get out of the way.

"You made my brother get gravel dings in his new paint," Kirk said, appearing unmoved by Caine's famous smile.

"And damned impolite of me it was, too," Caine agreed.

He knew Harmon's fury had little to do with a few paint dings. What had him all uptight was the fact that he felt he'd been made to look like a coward in front of his entire town.

Caine finally saw what Harmon had tattooed on his arm. It was an amazingly accurate facsimile of a Peterbilt log truck.

Not an encouraging sign.

"So, naturally, I have every intention of paying for any damage I may have—"

He was reaching into the back pocket of his jeans for his wallet, when Harmon let out a roar, lowered his gray head and charged like an enraged buffalo, butting an unprepared Caine in the gut.

The air whooshed out of Caine's body. "D-dammit, H-H-Harmon," he gasped. "We c-c-can w-work this out."

He saw a burly fist coming and ducked just in time. Caine heard the air whiz past his ear. "I take it that's a n-no."

Someone—Kirk probably, since Harmon was standing in front of him—hit Caine a thunderous blow on the side of his head. As he lurched around on wobbly legs, Caine managed to get the heel of his hand under Harmon's pug nose and rammed upward.

When Harmon cried out in pain, Kirk grabbed a handful of Caine's hair and sent him sprawling. He skidded across the floor, coming up the way he used to pull out of a slide.

By now the entire room was in motion. Johnny Duggan left his stool as if ejected from it, with Joe Bob and Tom and Dana Anderson right behind. Other men followed.

Some, due to family loyalty along with a few others envious of Caine's fame, sided with the Olson boys. The others remained loyally in Caine O'Halloran's camp.

Caine, on the floor with his face in the sawdust, felt a steel-toed boot slam into his ribs. Flashbulbs exploded in his head behind his eyes, and his stomach roiled.

Enraged, he staggered to his feet, and while the Anderson brothers kept Kirk occupied, Caine slugged away at Harmon, resorting to the boxing techniques he'd learned in college.

Right jab, left cross. Right jab, left cross. Harmon suddenly lurched. Watching him fall to the ground, Caine had a perverse urge to call out "Timber!"

"All right, goddammit, that's enough!"

Oley took out the shotgun he kept beneath the bar for just such occasions and fired it into the air. Loaded with blank shells, it managed to silence the room without causing undue damage to the smoke-covered ceiling.

"You boys have had your fun. Now why don't you just sit down and get back to drinkin' before I have to start writin' out bills for broken furniture."

Harmon staggered to his feet. Caine, braced against the bar, held his fists up in front of him, Joe Sullivan-style.

To Caine's surprise, Harmon thrust out a bruised hand. "I'm willin' to call a truce if you are."

Immensely grateful for the furious giant's abrupt about-face, Caine accepted the gesture of reconciliation. As he reached out to shake Harmon's outstretched hand, Kirk hit Caine with something a great deal larger and heavier than a fist.

A red haze covered Caine's eyes, a gong reverberated inside his head. And then he went down.

When he opened his eyes again, his mouth was full of sawdust and his head was swimming.

"Caine? You okay?" The man's voice sounded as if it were coming from the bottom of the sea. "Dammit, boy, answer me," Joe Bob urged.

Caine pushed himself up onto his hands and knees. He stayed that way, his head hanging like a winded horse for a long time, trying not to embarrass himself by throwing up.

Johnny Duggan squatted down beside him. When he put his broad hand on Caine's shoulder, Caine flinched. "Want me to go for the doctor?" Johnny asked.

"No." Caine closed his eyes and took a few deep breaths. When he opened them again, he could focus a little more clearly. His shirt was wet and he reeked of whiskey. "I'm okay."

He crawled over to a nearby table, grabbed hold of a heavy oak chair and slowly pulled himself upright. The sea of faces staring at him blurred for a minute.

Caine inhaled again, which cleared his vision, but made his chest feel as if it were on fire. Glancing around the bar, he saw, with relief, that the Olson boys were gone.

"What happened to the gorillas?"

"After Kirk sucker-hit you with that bottle, Oley threatened to call the sheriff. That's when they decided they had other things to do," Joe Bob explained.

The bottle explained why he smelled like a drunk coming off a three-week-long bender, Caine decided. He tentatively felt his mouth with his left hand. It was swollen and his lip was cut, but no teeth appeared to be loose. And his nose, thankfully, seemed to be okay, too.

"You know, Caine, you are whiter than new snow," Tom Anderson said.

"Not to mention your pretty face lookin' like Joe Bob's catcher's mitt," his brother Dana added. "And you're swaying on your feet like an old-growth hemlock about to fall. Come on, hotshot," he said, taking hold of Caine's arm. "Let's get you over to the clinic."

"You've got a clinic here now?" Caine was grateful for that bit of news. The way his stomach was churning, he didn't think he could take driving down those twisting mountain switchbacks to the hospital at Port Angeles. "Since when?"

"Since Nora came back from the Bronx six months ago and opened one up in Gram's old house," Tom answered.

Propped up by the Anderson brothers, Caine had been making his way, painful step by painful step, toward the door. At this latest bulletin, he stopped in his tracks. "I don't think this is a very good idea, guys."

"Try looking in a mirror and telling us that," Tom advised.

"You don't have to worry about a thing," Johnny Duggan assured Caine. "The girl turned out to be a right fine doctor. Fixed up my yella-jacket stings just fine. Should be able to patch you up without any trouble at all."

"I'm fine," Caine said, trying to ignore the flames licking at the inside of his chest. "All I need is a stiff drink and a little rest."

"You need to be checked out," Dana corrected. Under his breath, he added, "Don't worry, Caine. From what we can tell, Nora's put the past behind her."

If that was true, Caine wondered what the chances of his ex-wife passing on her secret might be. Not good. Since despite her brother's optimistic assertion, Caine couldn't forget her pale face and ice-cold eyes when she'd told him that she'd never—ever!—forgive him for their son's death.

"I still don't think..." His head fogged again; he took another breath to clear it. "Aw, hell."

Dana Anderson watched the color fade from Caine's battered face, saw the pain in his eyes and made his decision. "You're going to have to face her sometime, Caine," he said, pushing open the door. "Might as well get it over with."

3

IT HAD BEEN A LONG DAY. Twenty minutes after her last patient had departed, an exhausted Nora was getting ready to close the office when the clinic door opened, and there, standing in the doorway, haloed by a blaze of light from the setting sun behind him, was Caine O'Halloran.

His handsome face had been badly battered, his upper lip was split open and his right eye was surrounded by puffy flesh the color of ripe blueberries. He was weaving in the doorway, braced on either side by two rugged blond men she knew too well.

How dare her brothers go drinking with Caine! And then, to have the unmitigated gall to bring him here, expecting her to patch him up after whatever drunken brawl he'd gotten into this time, was really pushing their luck!

Although his right eye was swollen almost completely shut, the left was as blue as a morning glory and gleamed with a devilish masculinity that long ago—in another world, at another time—had possessed the power to thrill her.

Caine's split lip curved in a boyish grin that Nora knew had coaxed more than his share of women into sharing intimate favors.

"I sure hope you weren't planning to close up shop early, Doc," he greeted her in his deep, bedroom voice. "Because you just got yourself another patient."

It was as if time had spun backward, and Caine and her brothers were boys again. Having gone through their wild years together, the unholy trio had gotten in more than their share of fights. They'd always emerged, bloody but not bowed, grinning with the sheer satisfaction of having stuck up for one of their own.

"Dana Anderson, I thought you'd grown up." Nora turned on him, not yet prepared to confront Caine. "And exactly how do you plan to explain that black eye to Karin?" she asked Tom hotly.

He shrugged, looking sheepish. "I don't suppose you'd be willing to back me up if I told her that I got hit with the wrong end of a two-by-four."

"You're right. I wouldn't." Nora turned her back and walked into the examining room.

The three men exchanged an uneasy look, then followed.

"But it wouldn't do you any good even if I was willing to lie," she continued as she opened a small refrigerator and took out a cold pack, "since by breakfast tomorrow, everyone in town will know that the Anderson boys were out brawling with that hellion, Caine O'Halloran.

"Here." She tossed the gelled pack to her brother. "Put this on that eye. It'll be ugly as sin by morning, but that should help keep the swelling down."

She took her other brother's hands and frowned as she looked at his skinned knuckles. "This is going to hurt for at least a week," she predicted.

"You don't have to sound so pleased about it," Tom complained.

"It's only what you deserve for fighting. And at your age!"

"You saying we should have let the Olson boys kill Caine?"

"I'm saying that responsible men—intelligent adult males with wives and children—don't get into brawls in bars."

She shot Caine a cool, disapproving glance, really looking at him for the first time since the men had entered the clinic.

"I'm not surprised that you're involved in this." Her voice reminded Caine of the ice on a melting glacier—cold and dangerous. "One day back in town and you're already in trouble."

"Harmon swung the first punch, Nora," Dana said.

She arched a blond brow. "And I wonder whatever could have provoked him? Could it be, perhaps, that some hotshot jock with an IQ smaller than his neck size practically killed Harmon by playing chicken in a Ferrari in some misguided attempt to live up to his stupid macho image?"

"Ouch," Caine objected. "What the hell ever happened to Osler's creed—the part about a doctor judging not, but meting out hospitality to all alike?"

Sir William Osler had been a famous clinician in the late-nineteenth and early-twentieth centuries. Enthusiastic about his theories concerning the emotional and social responsibilities of a physician, Nora had quoted from his essays to Caine. At the time, he'd been so busy rubbing some foul-smelling grease on his damn glove, she hadn't thought he'd heard a word she'd said.

"I'm amazed you remember that." Surprise took a bit of the furious wind out of her sails.

"Oh, I remember everything about those days, Nora," Caine answered quietly.

An uncomfortable silence fell over the room. "Well," Dana said with forced enthusiasm, "now that Caine's in your expert hands, little sister, I guess I'll get back to work."

"And I promised Karin I'd stop and pick up some milk and bread on the way home," Tom said.

Caine grinned, then flinched when it hurt his split lip. "Chickens."

Dana didn't deny it. "Cluck, cluck," he said instead. "Don't be too rough on him, Nora. Those Olsons have always fought dirty."

"Kirk hit Caine on the back of the head with a whiskey bottle when he was shaking hands with Harmon," Tom added.

"I suppose that explains why you smell like a distillery," Nora said, wrinkling her nose with obvious distaste.

"Take good care of him, sis," Dana said when Caine didn't answer.

Tom seconded the request and then they were gone, leaving Nora and Caine alone in a room that suddenly seemed too small for comfort.

"Well, I suppose we may as well get this over with," Nora said with a decided lack of enthusiasm. "Wait here while I get some ice for that eye."

"I'd rather have a cold pack like the one you gave Dana."

"Tough. We had a run on cold packs today. That was my last one."

She left the room, expecting Caine to remain where he was. Instead, he followed her to the kitchen where, in the old days, he and Tom and Dana and sometimes a young, bespectacled Nora—who'd usually had her nose stuck in a book—had sat around the table, eating cookies and drinking milk from Blossom, Anna Anderson's black-and-white cow.

Rosy red strawberries still bloomed on the cream wallpaper, shiny copper pans continued to hang from a wrought-iron rack over the island butcher-block table.

The long pine trestle table was the same, although now, instead of plates of cookies and glasses of milk, its scarred and nicked surface was covered with medical books, suggesting that Nora still read while she ate. The ladder-back chairs that he remembered being dark blue had been repainted a bright apple green; one was missing.

"I can almost smell bread and cookies baking," he said.

"Things change," Nora replied as she filled an ice pack with cubes from the double-door refrigerator-freezer.

"Tell me about it," he muttered. "I was honestly sorry when I got the letter from Dana telling me about your grandmother's stroke. She was a terrific lady. I liked her a lot."

"Gram always liked you, too." Her curt tone indicated that she couldn't imagine why.

"Dana also said something about your parents having turned into gypsies."

"The day after Dad retired and turned the mill over to Tom, he came home with a motor home. Two weeks later, he and Mom hit the road.

"That was a year ago and they haven't settled down anywhere for more than six weeks. In fact, I got a call from them last week from someplace called Tortilla Flats, Arizona. They were on their way to Yellowstone Park through Monument Valley."

"I guess they're making up for lost time. I can't remember your dad ever taking a day off, let alone a vacation." Caine rubbed his chin, dark with the stubble of several days' growth of beard, thoughtfully. "Except for the day Dylan was born." And the day he'd died, Caine recalled grimly.

It was bad enough having Caine back in Tribulation.

She damn well didn't want to discuss her child with the man.

"Here." Nora shoved the ice pack at him. "If you're finished strolling down memory lane, I'd like to examine you."

Caine followed her, with uncharacteristic meekness, back down the hall to what had been her grandmother's front parlor.

Now designed for efficiency, rather than comfort, the formerly cozy room was dominated by an examining table, covered with fresh paper from a continuous roll. There was a short, wheeled, dark brown upholstered stool, a white pedestal sink and a small writing table. Beside the table was the ladder-back chair missing from the kitchen.

Instead of the fragrant potpourri Anna Anderson had made from the colorful blooms in her backyard rose garden, the room smelled vaguely of disinfectant and rubbing alcohol.

Beside the writing table, Anna's oak china cabinet, handmade by her husband, Oscar, had been turned into a supply cabinet. Behind the glass doors, the old crabapple-decorated plates had been replaced with boxes of dressings, plastic gloves, hypodermic syringes and shiny stainless-steel instruments.

A window looked out on Anna's rose garden and the woods; between the slats of the unfamiliar miniblinds, Caine saw a family of deer grazing, their brown and gray coats almost blending into the foliage behind them.

"Nora, look."

Surprised by his soft tone, she turned and glanced out the window. Her lips curved into a gentle, unconscious smile.

"They come every day about this time. Last Friday was the first day they brought the babies."

Caine squinted. "Where? I don't see any fawns."

"There are two of them. Beside that hemlock."

When Nora pointed, her fingers brushed against the rock-hard muscle of his upper arm. She pulled her hand back, as if burned.

Caine observed the telling gesture and decided not to comment on it. "I see them now." The creamy spots, nature's clever camouflage, had done their job well. "God, I've missed this," he said on a long deep sigh.

She glanced up at him, clearly surprised. "If you actually mean that, I'd better check out your head injury. All you ever used to talk about was how baseball was going to be your way out of Tribulation."

"I guess I did say that," Caine agreed reluctantly.

Trust Nora to remember that. He ran his hand through his hair and sighed again.

"But I don't know, when everything started falling apart, I found myself drawn back home. As if somehow, I'd find the answers I've been looking for here."

"Answers to what questions?"

"That's the hell of it. I don't know." He gave her a faint embarrassed smile. "I sound like Dorothy, don't I? 'Please, Almighty Wizard of Oz, I just want to go back home, to Kansas,'" he mimicked in a falsetto.

"Hell, maybe instead of driving the Ferrari back from New York, I just should have clicked my heels together and said, 'There's no place like home. There's no place like home.'"

"If you could've gotten home by clicking your heels, there wouldn't have been any reason for the Olson boys to beat you up," Nora added briskly. "Which brings me to your examination."

She washed her hands at the sink, then dried them with a paper towel. "So where does it hurt?"

"Everywhere," he answered promptly, holding the ice pack against his eye. "But I guess my chest and the back of my head feel the worst."

Cool, measuring eyes flicked over him. "Take off your shirt and jeans and get onto the table," she instructed. "Then we'll see how much damage you've done this time."

"It was Harmon and Kirk who did the damage," Caine felt obliged to say. "I offered to pay for any damage to Harmon's rig, but he wasn't having it."

"Perhaps that'll teach you that you can't buy everything you want," Nora suggested dryly. "Call me when you're undressed." She left the room, closing the door with a decided click.

Caine unbuttoned the bloodstained denim shirt and shrugged out of it, grimacing when the gesture caused a sharp pain in his chest. He managed, with difficulty, to pull off his boots, then his jeans.

Finally, clad solely in white cotton briefs and crew socks, wincing and swearing under his breath, he pulled himself up onto the examination table.

"Ready," he called out in the direction of the shut door.

Although the papers were reporting that Caine O'Halloran had reached the end of his playing days, Nora's first thought, when she returned to the room, was that her ex-husband's body was definitely not that of a man past his prime. He was exactly as Nora remembered him: all lean muscle and taut sinew.

He was also, for a fleeting moment, more than a little appealing. Pressing her lips together, she blocked that thought.

"You look as if you've been kicked by a mule."

Actually, he felt as if he'd been run over by an entire mule train, but Caine would have died before admitting that. "A mule probably would have been preferable to the Olson boys."

Reminding herself that she was a physician and this near-naked man was merely her patient, Nora began her examination with his head. The whiskey bottle had broken, causing a jagged laceration.

"You're going to need stitches."

"Why do I get the impression you're just looking for an excuse to stick a sharp instrument into my flesh?"

"Don't flatter yourself. Although infected scalp wounds are admittedly rare, when they do occur they're a real mess. Medically and cosmetically."

She gave him a dry, feigned smile. "And I'm sure you wouldn't want to permanently mess up that pretty head."

"You're the doctor," Caine said.

Despite the pain, which was considerable, all the beer he'd drunk during the afternoon had created a pleasant buzz that made this meeting with Nora less stressful than he'd expected.

"If you say I need stitches, who am I to argue?"

Who indeed? She couldn't remember a time when she and Caine hadn't argued. About everything. Well, perhaps not everything. The sex, once they'd abandoned her fought-for celibacy agreement, had admittedly been good. Better than good. Unfortunately, they hadn't been able to spend all their lives in bed.

She pulled her penlight out of the pocket of her lab coat. "Keep your head straight and follow the beam with your eyes."

His dark blue eyes moved to the left, then to the right, then up and down as she checked his pupillary reactions.

Although she had to lift the lid of the swollen eye to examine it, Nora found no interior damage.

Pocketing the light, she placed a hand on the back of his neck and ran her fingers over the series of bumps making up the cervical spine before going on to his chest.

"You're going to have some ugly body bruising."

So why didn't she tell him something he didn't know? "You should see the other guy."

Frowning at his flippant attitude, Nora put the bell of her stethoscope against his battered chest. The whooshing breathing sounds were a good sign that a rib hadn't punctured a lung, which was a possibility, considering the strength of the Olson boys.

"Tell me if anything hurts." She pressed his left shoulder with her fingertips, but received no response. She moved her fingers over his left nipple and pressed.

Her hands were pale and slender, her fingers long and tapered, her nails neat and unpolished. Caine remembered a time when those soft hands had moved with butterfly softness against his chest; now, her touch remained strictly professional as it probed for injuries.

When her fingers moved over his ribs, she hit a hot spot, causing Caine to suck in a quick breath. She pressed again.

"Does this hurt?"

Sadist. He decided she was probably gouging her fingers into him just to make him suffer. "It's not exactly a love pat, sweetheart," he said through gritted teeth.

"We'll need to take an X ray. It's probably just a cracked rib, but I don't want to take a chance on it being broken and puncturing a lung."

"I don't really feel up to driving to Port Angeles, Nora."

"You don't have to. Last month I would have called an

ambulance, but you're in luck, O'Halloran. My new portable X-ray machine arrived last week."

"I'm impressed."

Although he had no idea what such a piece of medical equipment cost, Caine suspected that it wasn't cheap. If she'd made such a major investment, she was obviously planning to stay in Tribulation.

Which, Caine decided, probably wasn't all that surprising. Nora had always loved it here on the peninsula; he'd been the one anxious to move on to bigger and better—meaning more exciting—things.

"I figured it would come in handy for broken arms, cracked ribs, the sort of occupational and recreational injuries I get a lot of," Nora said. "But I guess everyone's been extra careful, because not one patient has come in with a proper excuse for me to use it."

"Then I suppose that makes this all worthwhile," he declared. He brushed his hair away from his brow; as always, it fell untidily back again. "Anything to oblige a lady."

His voice was a low sexy drawl, with a hint of mockery. His eyes, dark and knowing, roamed her face with the intimate impact of a caress.

Nora's hand was still on his chest; she could feel his strong steady heartbeat beneath her fingertips. An unexpected, unbidden awareness fluttered between them. A lull fell as they studied each other.

Her hair, which he remembered her wearing in a long braid that hung down her back like a thick piece of pale rope, had been cut to a length that just brushed her shoulders, curving inward to frame her face. The naturally blond strands glistened like sunshine on fresh snow.

Nora Anderson's eyes, unlike those of the rest of her family, whose eyes were the expected Scandinavian blue, were a soft doe brown. One of her few concessions to vanity was to darken the double layer of thick blond lashes surrounding them.

Caine's gaze drifted down to the delicately molded lips that she was still forgetting to color. Although he knew it was ridiculous, he imagined that he could taste those soft lips, even now.

Desire spread, then curled tightly, like a fist in his gut, as Caine remembered those long-ago nights, when Nora's body, rounded with child, had moved like quicksilver beneath his. He remembered her mouth—warm, soft, avid—and the way she'd murmur his name—like a prayer—after their passion had finally been spent.

As Caine silently studied her, Nora tried not to be affected by the way an unruly lock of sun-streaked sandy brown hair fell across his forehead, contrasting vividly with his dark tan. A purple bruise as dark as a pansy bloomed on his lower jaw; his square chin possessed a stubborn masculine pride that bordered on belligerence. His arms were strong, with rigid, defined tendons, his shoulders were broad, his battered chest well muscled.

His washboard-flat stomach suggested that all the drinking and carousing she'd been reading about in the papers lately was a newly acquired bad habit. Knowing how hard Caine had worked to mold his naturally athletic body to this ideal of masculine perfection, she couldn't imagine her ex-husband ever succumbing to a beer gut.

Her gaze followed the arrow of curly hair that disappeared below the waistband of his white cotton briefs with an interest that was distressingly undoctorlike.

Although she knew it was dangerous, and warned herself against it, for a long humming moment Nora, too, was remembering the fever that had once burned between them.

His head wound began to bleed again. She jammed a sterile dressing on it. "Hold this steady," she directed. "And lie down."

She continued examining him with more force than necessary, making him flinch again. "You did that on purpose."

"So file a complaint with the State Medical Board," she snapped. "I think you're going to live," she decided after more probing and poking. "Let's take some pictures of that rib."

He accompanied her into the adjoining room, where she donned a lead apron. "Stand with your chest against this plate. Hands out to your sides."

"I'll have to let go of the bandage."

"I realize that. But that wound is far from fatal." She made an adjustment to the bulky machine. "Now, when I tell you, take a deep breath and hold it."

They both knew taking such a breath was bound to be painful. "I don't remember you being so sadistic."

"That's funny—" she took hold of his shoulders and straightened his torso "—I could swear that, just a little while ago, I heard you say that you were a man who remembered everything.... Don't move."

She made another adjustment, then checked her controls. "Okay, hold absolutely still. I'm ready to shoot."

"Nora?"

"What now?"

"Do you think you could use another word? That particular one doesn't give me a great deal of confidence."

When a reluctant smile crossed her lips, Nora pressed them together. Hard.

"Shut up, O'Halloran. And don't you dare move." She stepped just outside the open doorway. "Take a deep breath. That's it. Now hold." The X-ray machine whirred, then clicked.

"Go on back to the examining room," she said briskly after she'd taken two more views. "I'll be with you in a minute."

Caine wanted to ask Nora if she'd ever thought of using the word *please*, decided that there wasn't any point in aggravating her further, and did as instructed.

He sat on the edge of the examining table, legs dangling over the side, and gazed around the room.

The walls were a soft pale green reminiscent of new fir needles in the spring. The ceiling was the color of freshly churned cream. Diplomas, framed in oak, attested to her professional competence.

It did not escape Caine's notice that the name calligraphically inscribed on all those diplomas was Dr. Nora Anderson. Not that he was surprised; neither of them had ever really thought of her as Mrs. Caine O'Halloran.

"All right," she said as she returned to the room. "Let's see what we've got here."

She snapped the X-ray film onto a light box. When she flicked on the switch, the film went from all black to shades of gray. "Just as I thought." Nora nodded with satisfaction. "You've got a cracked rib."

"You don't have to sound so pleased."

"I'm far from pleased when I get a patient who risks his health—not to mention his life—due to stupidity," she flared. "If Harmon had broken that rib instead of merely cracking it, it could have punctured a lung."

"He attacked me, Nora," Caine reminded her. "I really didn't have any choice."

"You made your choice when you decided to play chicken with him on the highway," she pointed out. "That was an idiotic, childish thing to do."

Caine shrugged, then wished he hadn't when a lightning bolt zigzagged through his chest. "It seemed like a good idea at the time."

"If you keep up these adolescent acts of derring-do, Caine O'Halloran, you're going to end up in the morgue."

"Nice bedside manner you've got there, Dr. Anderson."

Ancient animosities, never fully dealt with, surfaced. "If you want an acquiescent female hovering at your bedside, kissing your owies to make them better, I'd suggest you get in that Ferrari and go home to your wife."

Nora examined the wound on the back of his head, then began cleansing the cut with sterile saline and dilute soap.

"I'm not married."

She tugged on a pair of surgical gloves. "That's not what I hear."

"All right, I guess we're technically married, but Tiffany—who, by the way, never let marriage interfere with her constant need for male companionship—is currently sleeping with one of my old teammates. She's also filed for divorce."

He frowned, thinking of his last conversation with his New York lawyer. Tiffany was insisting that six months of marriage entitled her to half of his last contract earnings. While Caine had been willing to pay it, writing his second marriage off as an expensive mistake, his attorney had counseled restraint.

"Apparently, an up-and-coming outfielder is socially more desirable than a relief pitcher who's been put out to pasture on waivers."

"I'm sorry," Nora said, meaning it.

"I can't really blame her," Caine said. "I knew all along that Tiffany was only along for the ride. So, I can't expect her to tag along if that ride takes a downhill turn on the way."

He didn't add that since his injury, he'd been a less-than-ideal husband. He'd been, by turns, sullen, uncommunicative, hot-tempered and angry. And those unappealing mood swings hadn't been helped by his increased drinking.

But dammit, Caine had told himself innumerable times in an attempt to justify his behavior over these past months, given the choice of sitting home and listening to his young, spoiled, self-centered bride whine about how she'd never agreed to be the wife of a washed-up old has-been, or going out to some convivial watering hole, where people still treated him like a hero, he'd choose the drinks and his newfound friends any day.

"Nice view of matrimony you've got there, O'Halloran," Nora murmured.

Caine shrugged. "Hell, Nora, you know as well as I do that marriage is nothing more than a convenient deal between two people who both have something the other wants. So long as things stay the same, the relationship putters along okay.

"But let the balance of power shift, and it's over. Finished. Kaput."

Nora thought back on the unromantic agreement she'd forged with Caine on that long-ago rainy afternoon. Their marriage had admittedly started out as a convenient deal to legitimize an unborn child's birth. But surprisingly, for a too-brief, shining time, it had blossomed into something more. And then it was gone, disappearing back into the mists of memory like the fabled Brigadoon.

"What about love?" The minute she heard the quiet words escape her lips, she wished she could take them back.

"Hell, if there's one thing life has taught me, sweetheart, it's that love is nothing more than good sex tied with pretty words."

Caine's cynical view of love and marriage, along with his wife's seeming desertion, had Nora almost feeling sorry for him.

"Well, I wouldn't worry about being alone for long, O'Halloran," she said as she drew up some Xylocaine into a syringe. "If that nude layout in this year's *Playgirl* calendar was an advertisement for wife number three, you should get a lot of applicants."

Caine felt the bite of the needle and drew in a short, painful breath. "You've seen it?"

Caine couldn't imagine, in his wildest dreams, this woman even glancing at a *Playgirl* calendar. Then he remembered how, before their marriage and their lives had fallen apart, Nora had displayed a fire he'd never suspected was under all that Scandinavian ice.

"Hasn't everyone?" She put in a stitch, tied it, then moved on to the next one.

"Well?"

"Well, what?" She made another careful stitch.

"What did you think?" He pressed his hand against his stomach in a futile attempt to quiet the giant condors that were flapping their wings harder with each stitch Nora made. "Have I still got it?"

"I suppose you'll do. In a pinch."

"You always were so good for the ego," Caine muttered. "And for the record, I wasn't naked."

Nora scraped at the sides of the wound with a fine scalpel, straightening the jagged edge. "From the way you were holding your glove in front of your vital statistics, you looked pretty naked to me."

Caine glanced into the mirror, saw what she was doing,

felt his stomach lurch and looked away. "I suppose, to be perfectly honest, I was advertising, in a way. But not for a new wife.

"Although I didn't admit it to the press until I got put on waivers," Caine said, "I knew all along that I wasn't going to be starting this season. That being the case, my agent felt we needed to keep my name in front of the public."

"I suppose I can understand keeping your name alive," Nora said, "but where does taking off all your clothes and posing with a baseball mitt and a cocker spaniel come in?"

"Hey, I sure as hell wouldn't be the first athlete to use a calendar or a sexy photo shoot to show he's still in shape," Caine argued. "It's the same thing all those actresses do to prove to producers and casting directors that they're not over the hill.

"As for the spaniel, that was the photographer's idea. She said something about a cute dog making me look both tough and soft at the same time.

"Besides, at least the calendar and all the press it generated was a helluva lot better than all those stories the sports reporters are writing about me being a washed-up, out-of-shape old wreck."

"It's fortunate you didn't get yourself beaten up before that photo shoot," Nora said. "Because right now you are anything but photogenic."

She finished the last three stitches, then pulled off the gloves and tossed them into the white enamel trash can.

"That's it?" Caine asked, not quite able to conceal his relief. Although she'd done a pretty good job of killing the pain, the sound of the silk thread pulling through his numb flesh had made him queasy.

"That's it." When she turned around, Nora caught him

surreptitiously rubbing his hand. "Let me see that." She took hold of the hand that had always been so much larger and darker than her own. "Dammit, Caine, your knuckles look worse than Tom's."

"I was just grateful your brothers were there to help me."

"They always were." His knuckles were badly bruised, and skinned, but nothing was broken, Nora determined.

"The Three Musketeers," Caine remembered fondly.

She turned his hand over. "You're still shaving your fingers."

"Hey, as a doctor, you use your best tools. Well, my fingers are my tools and shaving a layer of skin off my fingertips gives me an ultrasensitive touch."

She'd been three months pregnant, and a reluctant new bride, when she'd first found him using a surgical scalpel on his fingertips. She'd accused him of barbaric behavior, but months later, when they'd finally consummated the marriage neither of them had wanted, she'd been unwillingly stimulated by the idea of his heightened tactile sensitivity.

Memories, painful and evocative, hovered between them. Caine's eyes moved to the front of her white lab coat, remembering how her breasts felt like ripe plums in his hands.

Nora remembered the way his compelling midnight blue eyes seemed to darken from the pupils out when he was aroused.

Caine wondered if there was a man in Nora's life now. And if so, if they did all those things together that he'd taught her to do with him.

"I read that you've lost the feelings in your fingers," Nora ventured finally, seeking something—anything—to say.

"The feeling's come back," Caine insisted, not quite truthfully. "I just have a little control problem."

"Well, I wish you luck. Sensor-motor injuries are unpredictable. Who knows, you may actually prove all the naysayers wrong and be back on the mound by the All-Star break."

Which would, of course, result in yet another injury. Although Nora had never been a baseball fan, one of the few things she'd learned about the sport was the tradition of wearing out relief pitchers rather than starters.

The better a relief pitcher was—and Caine was undeniably one of the best—the more often a manager used him. Add to that the mental stress that came with pitching when the game was on the line, and it was no wonder relief pitchers tended to be men capable of living for the moment.

Needless to say, Nora had never been able to understand the appeal of such a life.

"I want to tape that rib. Then we'll be done." She wrapped a wide flesh-colored tape around his torso, tugging it so tightly he was forced to suck in a painful breath. "You can get dressed now," she said in the brisk, professional tone he was beginning to hate.

Without giving him a chance to answer, she left the room, closing the door behind her.

Caine braced his elbow on his bare thigh and lowered his head to his palm. The beer buzz was beginning to wear off and now, along with the pounding in his head, the ache surrounding his swollen eye, the crushing feeling in his chest and a grinding nausea, he was experiencing another all-too-familiar, almost-visceral pain.

"Damn," he muttered. "Maybe I shouldn't have come home, after all."

But he had, and now it was too late to get back in the

Ferrari and drive away. One reason he couldn't leave Tribulation was that having already cracked open Pandora's box, Caine knew that all the old hurts, ancient resentments and lingering guilt would eventually have to be dealt with.

The other and more pressing reason was that as much as he hated to admit it, Caine O'Halloran, hotshot baseball star and national sports hero, had absolutely nowhere else to go.

He dressed with uncharacteristic slowness, every movement giving birth to a new pain.

Nora was standing behind the oak counter she'd had built in the foyer, waiting for him.

"You'll need another appointment." She began leafing through the open appointment book. "If you're still in town two weeks from today, you can come in around four-thirty. Otherwise, you'll need to find another doctor to take out those stitches."

"Sorry to disappoint you, Doc, but I'm going to stick around for a while."

"And exactly how long is 'a while'?"

"You asking for professional reasons? Or personal ones?"

"Professional." She practically flung the word in his face.

Caine started to shrug, experienced another sharp stab of pain and decided against it. "Just wondering. And to answer your solely professional question, I'm sticking around for as long as it takes."

Nora didn't quite trust the look in his eyes. "For the feeling to come back in your fingertips?"

"Yeah." Caine nodded, his gaze on hers. "That, too."

When the mood threatened to become dangerously intimate once again, Nora became briskly professional, which was no less than Caine expected. "That'll be thirty-five dollars."

"Not exactly city rates."

"Tribulation is not exactly the city."

"Point taken."

It took a mighty effort, but he managed to pull his wallet out of his back pocket without flinching and withdrew a ten, a twenty and a five-dollar bill.

"You're in a hurry." He remembered this as she began filling out an insurance form. "I don't need a receipt."

"My accountant yells bloody murder if I don't keep accurate records," she said, signing her name to the form with a silver ballpoint pen. Her penmanship, Caine noted, was as precise as everything else about the woman. And even as he reminded himself that such painstaking attention to detail was simply Nora's nature, there was something about the meticulous cursive script that provoked the hell out of him.

She ripped the form apart, handed him the yellow and pink copies and kept the white one for herself. "Where are you staying?"

"At the cabin."

"All alone?"

"That's the plan."

"You might have a concussion. It'd be better if someone kept an eye on you."

"I don't have a concussion, Nora."

Her brow arched in the frostiest look she'd given him thus far. "Now you're a doctor?"

"No. But I've had concussions before, and I think I'd recognize one."

"You've drunk a lot today," she reminded. "All the alcohol is probably numbing the pain. You really should spend the night at your folks' house."

"I'm staying at the cabin. Alone."

"Still as hardheaded as ever, I see."

"Not hard enough," he countered.

"You'll have pain."

"I'm used to that."

"I'm sure you are. However, I'm still going to prescribe something to help get you through the night and the next few days."

"I can think of something a lot better than pills to help me get through the night."

The seductive suggestion tingled in the air between them.

Nora reached for the prescription pad. "Take one tablet, with food or a glass of water, every six hours as needed."

Her voice, Caine noted, had turned cold enough to freeze the leafy green Boston fern hanging in the front window. "Needless to say, you shouldn't drink and I wouldn't advise driving or operating heavy machinery."

"Damn. Does that mean I can't down the pills with a six-pack, then go to the mill and play Russian roulette with the ripsaw?"

She absolutely refused to smile. "Not if you want to keep that hand." She glanced at her watch as she tore off the prescription and handed it to him. "Nelson's Pharmacy should be open for another five minutes. I'll call ahead just in case his clock and mine aren't in sync."

Caine plucked the piece of white paper from her fingers and stuffed it into the pocket of his jeans without looking at it. "Thanks. I appreciate everything you've done."

"I'm a doctor, Caine. It's my job."

"True enough. But I've become painfully familiar with doctors, Nora, and believe me, none of them have as nice a touch as yours." He flashed her the bold, rakish grin that had added just the right touch to his calendar portrayal of Mr. April.

"If you don't behave, I'm going to call your mother to take you home."

"Why do I get the feeling you still refuse to put athletes in the same category as adults?"

"If the jockstrap fits..."

Her smile was patently false as she picked up the telephone receiver and began to dial. "You'd better get going, Caine. Ed Nelson isn't going to keep his pharmacy open all night. Even for the great local hero, Caine O'Halloran.

"Oh, hi, Ed, this is Nora. Just fine, thanks. And how are you? And Mavis? Another grandchild? Twins? You and Mavis must be thrilled. What does that make now, six? Eight? Really? Well, that's wonderful....

"The reason I called, Ed," Nora said, breaking into the pharmacist's in-depth description of the newest additions to the Nelson family, "is that I know it's near your closing time, but I'm sending a patient over."

She turned her back, studiously ignoring Caine.

Frustrated and aching practically everywhere in his body, Caine stalked to the door, then slammed it behind him with such vehemence that one of her diplomas fell off the wall in the adjoining room.

4

CAINE PICKED UP THE prescription at Nelson's Pharmacy and endured a lengthy conversation with the elderly druggist, who wanted to know all the particulars of Caine's career-threatening injury.

After finally escaping the medical interrogation, he stopped at the market, picked up cold cuts for dinner and, ignoring Nora's medical advice, purchased a couple of six-packs of Rainier beer. Just to take the edge off.

Then he drove out to the cabin—a cabin that, despite his avowal never to return to Tribulation, he'd never quite gotten around to selling.

Although he'd hired a woman from town to clean the place occasionally, the air was musty and a layer of dust covered everything. Caine neither noticed nor cared.

He turned on the television and tuned in to a game between Kansas City and Toronto on ESPN, threw himself down on the sofa, creating a dusty cloud, and pulled the tab on one of the blue metallic cans of beer. Foam spewed across the back of his hand; Caine licked it off his skin and settled back, stretching his legs out in front of him.

After swallowing two pink pills, he downed the entire can of beer in long thirsty chugs, tossed the can onto the pine coffee table, and opened another.

Three hours later, he'd made inroads on the beer and the Royals had shut out the Blue Jays at home, winning with a George Brett home run. And although the combination of pain medication and beer had created a pleasant, rather hazy buzz, he hadn't enjoyed the game.

The televised broadcast had driven home, all too painfully, the unpalatable fact that for the first time since his fourteenth summer, a new baseball season had begun without Caine O'Halloran on the mound.

That unpleasant thought kept him awake long into the night until, finally, the combination of drugs and alcohol allowed him to slip into a restless sleep.

CAINE WASN'T THE ONLY one who had difficulty sleeping. The following morning, Nora awoke more tired than she'd been when she went to bed and irritated with herself for letting Caine get under her skin. She'd tried to put him out of her mind, but ten-year-old memories, as vivid as if they'd occurred yesterday, had proved to be thieves of sleep.

She showered, blow-dried her hair and kept her makeup to a minimum of pink lipstick and mascara. Her clothing—pearl-gray skirt, matching blouse and low-heeled, comfortable shoes—was as subdued as her cosmetics. Although it was spring, mornings were chilly enough to require her wool coat.

As she gathered up her driving gloves, Nora cast a glance at the clock. If she left now, she could still make a stop before driving to Port Angeles.

The clouds were faint pink streaks in a pearly gray sky when Nora parked in front of the Tribulation Pioneer Cemetery. The small iron gate creaked as Nora pushed it open. The front rows of headstones, dating back to the founding of the town, were chipped and weather-pitted. An archangel guarding one resting place had been missing a wing for as long as she could remember.

Family plots were separated from the others by short

white picket fences; the older stones, made of marble or granite, were elaborately carved, the words chiseled into their surfaces lengthy tributes to the deceased. The newer graves were marked by slabs laid flat on the ground with only the name, dates, and a single line to denote a life now gone.

The white picket fence surrounding the Anderson family plot was kept gleaming by a fresh coat of paint applied by her father every June. This year the task would be passed on to Tom or Dana. The names on the stones went back five generations, to her Great-great-grandfather Olaf.

Nora could have made her way to the grave blindfolded.

Dylan Kirk Anderson O'Halloran, the simple marker stated. *Beloved son.* The inscribed dates told of a young life cut tragically short.

Each time she came to the grave, Nora hoped to find peace. The fact that she never found it never stopped her from coming.

Wildflowers were arranged in a metal cup buried in the ground beside the stone. The casual bouquet consisted of dainty purplish brown mission bells, lacy white yarrow, deep purple larkspur and cheery, nodding yellow fawn lilies. The flower petals glistened with dew.

The bouquet was silent testimony to the fact that Ellen O'Halloran had made her weekly pilgrimage to the cemetery. There were times—and this was one of them—when Nora felt slightly guilty that she'd insisted her son be buried in the Anderson family plot, especially since no one could have loved Dylan more than his paternal grandmother.

But then she would remember how Caine had arrived at the cemetery obviously drunk and had humiliated both families by punching out the workman whose job it had been to lower the small, white, flower-draped coffin into the ground.

Nora pulled off her gloves, then knelt and ran a hand over the brown grass that covered her son.

Her worst fear, after they'd put her child into that cold ground, was that she'd forget his round pink face, the sound of his bubbly laugh, his bright blue eyes, his wide, melon-slice baby smile.

But that hadn't happened.

Nine years after his death, she could see Dylan as if he were sitting right here, propped up in the maple high chair etched with teeth marks from two generations of O'Halloran boys, his bowl of oatmeal overturned on his head, laughing uproariously at this new way to win his mother's attention.

Bittersweet memories whirled through her mind—the hours spent walking the floor with Dylan at night, an anatomy text in hand, naming aloud the names of the endocrine glands.

How many babies, she'd wondered at the time, were put to sleep with an original lullaby incorporating the two hundred and six bones of the skeletal system?

Nora knelt there for a long, silent time, tasting the scent of spring in the air. The morning light was a muted rosy glow. Delicate limbs of peaceful trees, wearing their new bright green leaves, arched over the grave.

In the distance, the sawtooth peaks of the Olympic Mountains emerged from a lifting blanket of fog; the upper snowfields caught the rose light of the sky and held it.

Somewhere not far away, Nora heard the sweet morning songs of thrush and meadowlark, then the chime of the clock tower, reminding her of other responsibilities, other children who might need her.

"Mama has to go." She traced her son's name with her fingertip. The bronze marker was morning-damp and cold, but Nora imagined it was Dylan's velvety cheek she was touching. "But I'll be back, Dylan, baby. I promise."

After placing a small white pebble beside the one undoubtedly left by Dylan's paternal grandmother, Nora left the grave site. The cold ache in her heart was familiar; she always experienced it whenever she visited the cemetery. But she could no more stay away than she could stop breathing.

So immersed was she in her own thoughts, Nora failed to notice the man who'd been watching her the entire time she'd been in the cemetery.

Caine leaned against the trunk of a tree, his arms crossed, silently observing his former wife.

A hangover was splitting his head in two, his body ached and the stitches in the back of his head had already begun to pull uncomfortably. But since he knew that he deserved the crushing pain, he wasn't about to complain.

He hadn't wanted to come to the cemetery today; indeed, he hadn't entered those gates since the day of the funeral. A day when he'd shown up drunk, causing Nora, in an uncharacteristic public display of temper, to screech at him like a banshee. Her black-gloved fists had pounded at his chest with surprising strength until her father and brothers had managed to pull her away.

It wasn't that Caine hadn't loved Dylan; on the contrary, the little boy had been the sun around which Caine's entire universe had revolved.

Which was one of the reasons he had never returned to the spot where they'd insisted on putting his son into the ground, never minding the fact that Dylan was afraid of the dark.

Caine had come to the cemetery this morning in an attempt to expunge the lingering pain, and was unsurprised when it hadn't worked. He'd been about to leave when, as if conjured up from his dark and guilty thoughts, Nora had appeared out of the morning mists, looking strangely small and heartbreakingly frail.

SHE WAS ON HER WAY back to her car when she saw Caine. He was standing half-hidden in the shadows. She stopped, but refused to approach him. If he wanted to talk, let him come to her.

They remained that way, Caine leaning against the tree, Nora standing straight and tense, like a skittish doe, poised to flee at the slightest threat of danger.

"Hello, Nora." His voice was deep and gruff and achingly familiar.

"Hello, Caine." Her voice was low and guarded. "How are you feeling this morning?"

"Like I've been run over by Harmon Olson's Peterbilt, then drawn and quartered. But, since I figure I probably deserve every ache and pain, I'm not complaining."

Caine looked, Nora considered, almost as bad as she felt. Which meant he looked absolutely terrible. His face, normally tanned, even in the dead of winter, was ashen. Lines older than his years bracketed his rigid, down-turned mouth.

His eyes were red-rimmed, his jaw was grizzled by a rough beard and his clothes looked as if he'd slept in them.

"Did you take the pain pills I prescribed?"

"Not this morning." He managed a faint smile. "The way I look at it, so long as I feel the pain, I know I'm still alive."

"That's an interesting philosophy. But I'm not certain it'll catch on."

"Probably not. I hope you don't think I'm following you."

She shrugged and slipped her bare hands into her coat pockets. "Are you?"

"Actually, I've been here about an hour."

"Oh. I didn't see your car."

"I walked." He'd hoped the fresh air would clear his head. It hadn't.

"But it's at least three miles."

"My arm might be giving me a little trouble, but the day I can't walk a few measly miles is the day I hang up my glove."

A thought flickered at the back of her mind, was discarded, then returned. "You brought the flowers."

"Guilty."

Part of her wanted to go back and snatch the wildflowers from her son's grave; another part reminded her that Dylan was Caine's son, too.

"That was very thoughtful of you."

"They were growing all around the cabin."

He pushed away from the tree with a deep sigh and moved across the brown grass until he was standing in front of her.

"I came out this morning and when I saw them blooming, I thought about the time we had that picnic—one of our few summer Sunday afternoons together—and how when I went back to the car to get the portable playpen, you turned your back for a second to get the potato salad out of the cooler, and when you turned around again, Dylan was gnawing on that handful of wildflowers."

Despite her medical training, she'd been frantic, worried the blossoms might be poisonous. It had been Caine who'd calmly taken the wilting flowers from their son's grubby fist and offered a favored teething cookie in return.

"I've never been able to look at wildflowers again without thinking of how pleased he looked with himself, with yellow pollen all over his nose, his mouth ringed with dirt, and that enormous smile of his," Nora murmured.

"All four of his baby teeth gleaming like sunshine on a glacier." A reminiscent smile softened Caine's features. "That was a pretty good afternoon, wasn't it? If we'd only had a few more days like that, we might still be together."

"Caine, don't..."

She combed a hand through her silky hair in a nervous, self-conscious gesture he remembered too well; Caine caught hold of her hand on its way back to her pocket. It was, he noticed, ice-cold.

"We have to talk about it, Nora."

"No." She shook her head, sending her hair flying out like a swirling ray of sunshine in the shaft of shimmering morning light. "We said everything we had to say to one another nine years ago. There's no reason to rehash painful memories."

"We were both hurting," he reminded her, his voice as tightly controlled as hers. "And we both said things we didn't mean." His pained eyes looked directly into hers and held. "Don't you think it's time we settled things?"

She jerked her hand from his and stiffened—neck, arms, shoulders. A thin white line of tension circled her lips. "As far as I'm concerned, things were settled when you got into that new flashy red Corvette the insurance company gave you and drove away and left me all alone."

To deal with our baby's death. She hadn't said the words aloud, but they hovered in the air between them.

"You didn't ask me to stay," Caine reminded her.

"Would you have?"

For some reason he would have to think about later, Caine chose to tell the absolute truth. "No. Probably not."

"I didn't think so."

"Let me put the question another way," he said. "If I'd asked you to come with me, would you have?"

Years of controlling her expression while examining patients kept Nora from revealing how the unexpected question startled her. "And leave medical school?"

"Correct me if I'm wrong, but I believe there are medical schools in California."

He had her there. Realizing that he'd just pushed her into a very tidy corner, Nora hedged. "It's a moot point. Because you never asked me to go to California with you."

"If I had, if I had said, 'Nora, I'm so heartsick about everything that's happened, come with me to Oakland and let's try to start over again,' what would you have said?"

"I might have gone."

It was a lie; she never would have left friends and family and her lifelong ambition to go chasing after Caine's dream. But she'd blamed him for so many years that old habits died hard.

Caine's wide shoulders slumped visibly. Nora had been unrelentingly, coldly angry after the accident, after their child's death.

She'd told him so many times, in both words and actions, how much she hated him, that Caine had never suspected that he might have, with extra effort, been able to break through all her pain and fury.

But at the time, even if he'd wanted to, he wasn't sure he would have had the strength to try. Because, although he suspected she'd never believe it, he had been numb with unrelenting grief and guilt.

"I guess I really blew it, then."

When he dragged his wide bruised hand over his face, Nora felt a distant twinge of guilt for lying to him and ignored it. His dark eyes were those of a man who'd visited hell and had lived to tell about it.

"I told you, Caine, it's in the past. Let's just let it stay there."

"Life would probably be a lot easier if the past could be forgotten, Nora," he said. "But I think we both know it can't be."

Before she could answer, the clock in the village square tolled again. "I'm sorry, Caine, but I can't discuss this right now. I'm going to be late for work, as it is."

Caine glanced down at the Rolex sports watch he'd never been able to afford when he'd been married to her. "It's not even seven."

"I know, but it's a long drive to Port Angeles, and there are a lot of trucks on the road this time of morning."

"You have another clinic in Port Angeles?"

"No, I'm working in the hospital emergency room three days a week in order to fund the Tribulation clinic."

"The emergency room?"

How can you bear it? The words were unspoken, but they hung in the air between them just the same.

The memory of those hours they'd spent outside the hospital emergency room, at opposite ends of the small, smoke-filled waiting room, anger and fear and hurtful pride keeping them from comforting one another, came flooding back.

"During my internship at Columbia Presbyterian, in New York City—"

"I know where Columbia Presbyterian is," Caine broke in. "I lived in New York, remember? Before the Yankees cut me."

She remembered being afraid she would run into him. She also remembered reminding herself that New York was an enormous city; the odds of seeing her former husband were astronomical. But that hadn't stopped her from getting an ulcer that had mysteriously cleared up after she'd returned to Tribulation.

"Well, anyway," she said, shaking off that uncomfortable memory, "when it came time for me to do my ER rotation, I was sick to my stomach all night. I'd been dreading it for weeks. In fact, I was seriously thinking of dropping out of medicine."

She fell suddenly silent and stared up at him, wondering what on earth had possessed her to tell him something she'd never admitted to another living soul.

She took a deep breath that should have calmed her but didn't. "Anyway, thirty seconds after I managed to drag myself into the ER, an elderly woman who'd been attacked in her bed by a man with a machete was brought in. She had put her arms up to protect herself and there was blood everywhere.

"We must've pumped in a ton of blood, but eventually she stabilized enough to be sent up to surgery."

"Did she make it?"

"Oh, yes. But I didn't find that out for weeks, because all day patients just kept pouring in: knife fights, bullet wounds, heart attacks, rapes...

"The triage nurses had the patients stacked up like planes over Kennedy airport and by the time I got to stop long enough to have a cup of coffee, I'd been on the run for eighteen hours and had another eighteen to go, but— and this is hard to explain—I felt really, really good."

"Adrenaline tends to do that to you," Caine agreed absently. He was trying to come to grips with the idea of cool, calm and collected Nora covered with a stranger's blood, surrounded by the bedlam that was part and parcel of a city-hospital emergency room. Nora treating bullet wounds? Ten years ago he would have found the idea preposterous. Obviously he'd underestimated his former wife.

"I suppose so. But it was more than adrenaline. I loved being part of a team and I loved the action. It was fantastic!"

A smile as bright as a summer sun bloomed on her face and lighted her eyes. Caine tried to remember a time she'd smiled like that at him when they'd been married and came up blank.

"You should do that more often." Unable to resist touching her, he reached up and ran his palm down her hair.

It was only a hand on her hair. An unthreatening, nonintimidating touch. So why did it make her mouth go dry and her heart skip a beat?

"Do what?"

"Smile. You have a lovely smile. No wonder your patients love you."

It was happening all over again. When she felt herself falling under Caine's seductive spell, Nora took a step backward. Physically and emotionally. "I really do have to go."

"You haven't finished the story."

"What story?"

"About your first day in the emergency room."

"Oh. Well, as I said, the rush was amazing. I was hooked. I applied for a residency, got it, and I've been working in emergency departments ever since."

"I wish we'd been living together that day," Caine surprised both of them by saying. "I would have liked sharing it with you."

"Please, Caine—"

"I'd like to hear more about your work, your life. Could I take you to dinner tonight?"

"I'm sorry, Caine, but I have paperwork to catch up on tonight."

"Tomorrow night, then."

"I'm sorry, but—"

"All right, how about lunch?"

"I'm sorry, but the answer's still no."

"Breakfast?"

"No."

"I want to see you again, Nora. Just to talk. That's all."

She combed her hand through her hair again and was appalled to find it trembling visibly. "I really don't think it's a good idea, Caine," she said gently, but firmly.

"Why not?"

"Because it would be too painful." She flared suddenly, causing the birds perched on the branches overhead to take flight in a loud flurry of wings.

"Perhaps that's all the more reason to talk about it," Caine suggested mildly. "If we can get everything out in the open once and for all, perhaps we can put it behind us."

"Do you truly think that's possible?"

"We'll never know if we don't try."

For a brief, foolhardy moment, Nora was honestly tempted.

"No," she decided. "I don't want to see you again, Caine. Not for dinner, or lunch, or breakfast, or just to talk."

Unaccustomed to failure, but not knowing how to salvage the situation, Caine decided he had no choice but to back away. "I guess I'll just have to wait and see you in a couple of weeks."

"Really, Caine—"

"So you can take the stitches out," he reminded her. "Unless you'd rather have me go to a doctor in Port Angeles."

"No." Her cheeks were flushed. "Of course I'll take them out. There's no reason for you to drive all that way."

"Fine. Well, I guess I'll be seein' you."

"Yes."

He knew it was the last thing she wanted, but some perverse impulse made him put his hand against the side of her cheek in a final, farewell caress.

"Goodbye, Nora."

"Goodbye, Caine."

Caine gave her one long, last look, and then he turned and walked back toward the gate.

He had only gone a few paces when she called out to him. "Caine?"

He turned back toward her. "Change your mind about breakfast?"

"No." She reached into her shoulder bag and pulled out the silver ballpoint pen and a small yellow pad. "But I thought you might like the name of a doctor at Seattle Samaritan who specializes in your type of injury."

"I've gone to more damn specialists than you can shake a bat at, Nora."

"One more opinion couldn't hurt." She wrote the name on a piece of paper and held it out to him. "And Dr. Fields is really very good."

Although he wasn't at all eager, Caine took the paper and shoved it into his pocket. "Thanks. I appreciate your concern."

She searched his tone for sarcasm and found none. "You're welcome. Good luck."

"Thanks."

A maniac was operating a chain saw behind his eyes and his stomach was roiling from the can of warm beer he'd tossed down for breakfast.

Hell, Caine thought as he crossed the cemetery. *Maybe I shouldn't have come home, after all.*

In small towns, time had a habit of standing still. When he'd made the decision to return to Tribulation, that trait had seemed a plus. With his career in shambles, he'd found himself instinctively drawn back to the one place where he was still a larger-than-life hometown hero.

But dammit, he hadn't counted on Nora having returned home, as well.

"Nothing's changed," he muttered, jamming his hands so hard into his pockets that they tore. Loose change fell to the still-brown grass underfoot and went ignored. "Not a goddamn thing."

Feeling more alone than he'd ever felt in his life, Caine walked back through the wrought-iron gates. Away from his son. And his wife.

5

ONE WEEK AFTER HER unexpected encounter with Caine in the cemetery, Nora pulled her car into her reserved parking space outside the Mount Olympus Hospital and realized that she couldn't remember a single mile of the just-completed drive. It was not a propitious omen for the day ahead.

Ever since Caine's return, her mind had been mired in the past, rerunning old scenes from her marriage like some late-night cable-television movie.

Marrying Caine when she'd discovered she was pregnant had seemed a logical, practical solution. The problem was, she'd never planned on falling in love with the only man who had ever had the power to break her heart.

The sun had risen, the sky was as bright as a washtub of the Mrs. Stewart's bluing her grandmother had always favored. Walking toward the hospital, she waved at a gardener who was energetically clipping away at the rhododendron bushes flanking the sidewalk. He grinned and waved back, his own enjoyment of the perfect spring weather obvious. The double glass doors of the emergency department opened automatically at her approach. Nora took a judicial glance around the well-lighted waiting room. The only persons there this morning appeared to belong to the same family.

An exhausted-looking woman rocked a cranky baby in a stroller; at her feet, a young boy ran a toy car across the green vinyl tile while making loud roaring sounds meant to emulate a Formula race car. Beside the woman, a red-haired girl sat reading a children's book of fairy tales.

The woman and the girl didn't bother to look up as Nora passed; the boy glanced at her with a decided lack of interest, then began running the plastic car noisily up the wall.

After exchanging brief greetings with Mabel Erickson, the emergency room clerk, Nora went into the doctors' locker room, changed into a pair of unattractive but practical unpressed green scrubs, and clipped on her ID.

"You're starting out slow," Dr. Jeffrey Greene, the doctor going off the night shift said, flipping through the aluminum clipboards. "We had a relatively quiet night. Some hotshot took a corner too fast on his Kawasaki and I spent two hours picking pieces of asphalt and gravel out of his arms and chest. His girlfriend took him home.

"EMS brought in a drug overdose." He frowned at this latest problem to have worked its way to the peninsula from the Puget Sound cities. "We stabilized him and sent him upstairs to ICU. The only patient currently in the place is a kid with night asthma who should be off the breathing machine any time. His mother's in the waiting room, waiting to take him home.

"And, for comic relief, just when the pizza guy showed up with dinner, a frantic mother brought in a three-month-old with spots. She swore he had measles." He shook his head with disgust. "I'll never figure out why people bring their kids to the emergency room at three in the morning with diaper rash."

"She was probably scared." Nora certainly remembered her own middle-of-the-night parenthood fears.

In medical school she'd been constantly reading about life-threatening diseases, then fearing that Dylan had contracted one of them whenever he became ill. One of the more embarrassing incidents had been when he'd come down with a high fever and wouldn't stop crying.

Positive that her son had meningitis, Nora had driven alone—Caine had been out of town on a road trip—through the dark streets to the hospital at two o'clock in the morning.

The doctor on call had examined the three-month-old baby, patted Nora paternalistically on the head and diagnosed an ear infection. An hour later, Nora had returned home with a bottle of antibiotic and a sense of relief mingled with an enormous dose of professional embarrassment.

"The pizza was cold by the time we got around to it," Dr. Greene complained. "At the next staff meeting I'm asking Administration about that microwave they've been promising us. What kind of ER doesn't have a microwave oven, this day and age?"

When Nora didn't answer what she took to be a rhetorical question, he continued. "So, there you go, Doctor. So far you're looking at a long boring day." He gathered up the pizza box and pop cans and tossed them into a nearby wastebasket. "But of course, the morning's still young so that'll undoubtedly change."

Nora knew that, only too well. For some reason no one had ever been able to figure out, emergencies invariably came in waves; things would be so quiet the medical staff would be in danger of falling asleep, then suddenly all hell would break loose.

After confirming that the asthma patient had been released, Nora returned to the office, sipped a cup of coffee and waited.

The peace was shattered twenty minutes later when the speaker in the Emergency Communications and Information Center came to life. At the same time, the beeper in her pocket went off with the high-pitched squeal of the trauma stat code.

"All emergency personnel, trauma stat!" the wall speaker blared. "Helipad, ETA two minutes. Helipad. Two minutes."

Nora was waiting on the roof, along with a nurse and an ER technician when the EVAC helicopter arrived. In order to avoid wasting critical time, the pilot brought the craft straight in, circling and descending at the same time. The moment the skids touched the ground, the pilot unpitched his rotor blades, flattening them so they no longer bit into the air.

Bending her head, Nora and the rest of the crew grabbed hold of the gurney and raced toward the side of the helicopter. The helicopter medic threw open the door, then undid the heavy web straps holding the passenger— a little boy—in place.

Four sets of hands lifted the boy, who was strapped to a fracture board, a pink plastic collar immobilizing his neck, onto the gurney. Telling him not to be afraid, the nurse put a green plastic oxygen mask over his face, then the crew pulled the gurney back across the roof at a dead run. The state police helicopter medic followed, service revolver bouncing awkwardly against his navy blue flight suit.

"This is Jason Winters," the medic informed the team as they entered the code room. "He's a four-year-old male who did a double gainer out of his two-story bedroom window and landed on a wooden deck.

"Was unconscious no more than two, maybe three minutes. He's alert, he can move all extremities, his pulse is one fifty-five, respiration twenty plus, blood pressure one ten over seventy and solid as a rock.

"His mother says there's nothing unusual in his medical history, no known allergies. She was the one who found Jason. A neighbor's driving her here. ETA twenty, thirty minutes.

"The father's a city cop. The police station was notified, but he hadn't arrived there from home yet. The desk sergeant promised to give him the message the minute he came in."

After thanking the medic for his concise report, Nora bent over the gurney and brushed the boy's hair away from his forehead with a gentle, maternal touch.

"Hello, Jason. I'm Dr. Anderson. Do you know where you are?"

"In the hospital?"

"That's right." Nora smiled. "And we're going to take very good care of you."

"I wanna go home," Jason wailed.

"I know. But first we need to check you out and make certain nothing's broken. Can you help us do that?"

"Why can't I just go home?" His face was so pale his freckles stood out in stark relief.

"You will. I promise. But not quite yet, sweetie. First we have to take a blood sample."

"I don't want no shots!" he screamed as the nurse began swabbing the crook of his slender arm.

"It'll only sting for a minute, honey," the nurse promised.

The scream escalated into high-pitched shrieks as the boy watched his blood filling the syringe. "No-o-o! I want my mommy. I wanna go ho-o-ome!"

Another nurse hooked him up to the EKG and Nora watched as the line jumped wildly on the monitor, then settled down to a rapid beat normal for a frightened child.

"If you don't untie me, I'm gonna tell my daddy on

you! He's a policeman and he'll come with his gun and arrest you!"

The shrieks slid back down the scale and became racking sobs that gave Nora confidence. Every wail, every cry, said that Jason's airway was unobstructed.

"We'll take the straps off real soon, Jason," Nora promised, "but first we need to take some pictures to make certain that you didn't hurt anything when you fell."

"I didn't fall," he corrected with four-year-old pride. "I was swinging on my web."

"Your web?"

The first nurse wrapped a blood-pressure cuff around his arm and hooked it to a monitor programmed to automatically inflate the cuff and read the patient's blood pressure every two minutes.

"My Spiderman web... Hey, what are you doing now?" Jason yelled when the nurse began cutting away at his Ninja Turtle pajamas. "You can't do that! My mommy just bought me these pajamas. She'll be really mad at me!"

"We need to examine you, Jason," Nora soothed. "I promise to tell your mommy that we're the ones who tore your pajamas, but first, can you be a very big boy and tell me where it hurts?"

Fifteen minutes later, when her examination uncovered merely a sprained wrist and a nasty bump on the head, and the X rays showed no spinal damage, Nora decided that Jason was not only a very loud little boy, he was also a very lucky one. Although children's bodies were amazingly resilient, they definitely weren't designed for two-story falls onto a solid-wood deck.

The nurse was writing his name on a plastic wristband when the ER clerk appeared at the door of the trauma room. "The boy's mother is here."

Through the door, Nora could see a pretty, obviously

distraught young woman. She was pacing in front of the reception desk, tracks of tears staining her cheeks while her hands mangled a tissue. The stark fear and dread Nora recalled all too well were written all over her face.

Nora remembered prayers, learned in childhood, tumbling through her head on that day nine years ago. Desperate, she had made deal after deal with God: If He'd only let Dylan live, she'd never raise her voice at him again; if He'd only allow her son to survive, she'd figure out some way to take enough time from her studies to watch "Sesame Street" and Mister Rogers with him. If only God would keep her baby from dying, she'd do anything. Anything!

Nora remembered desperately trying not to cry and strangely, succeeding. And then she remembered trying not to scream, when they'd told her that her baby had died, and failing.

After instructing Mabel to inform Mrs. Winters that she'd be right there, Nora slipped out the door and walked to the stainless-steel fountain. Water arced up in a shimmering silver stream; Nora took a long drink and an even longer breath. Then she walked back down the hall to the waiting room.

"Hello, Mrs. Winters." She offered a reassuring smile. "I'm Dr. Anderson. Jason's doctor."

"Where's Jason?" the haggard woman asked immediately. "Where's my boy?"

"He's still in the trauma room," Nora said. "With the nurses and other support staff. But he's awake and doing fine."

On cue, another scream came from the trauma room. "He's hurting! I need to be with him."

"I'm afraid it'll be a few more minutes before you can see him, Mrs. Winters."

"They wouldn't let me go in the helicopter with him, they took him away and now no one will let me see my son and I want to know why!"

Mrs. Winters's voice had the quiver and staccato rush that told Nora, who'd faced too many parents in similar circumstances, that she was on the verge of becoming hysterical.

Nora leaned forward and put her hand on the woman's arm. "I know you want the best care for Jason and that's what he's getting.

"Your son is being taken downstairs for a CAT scan. It's not painful, it's merely a three-dimensional X ray that'll tell us if Jason suffered any head or internal injuries from the fall." Another wail echoed down the hall.

"Oh, God." The woman's face mirrored the anguish that Nora knew must have been on her own that day nine years ago. "Why is he screaming like that?"

"Because he's angry and frightened. And although I know how difficult it is to believe, Jason's crying is a very good sign. We've been reassured by every shriek."

Mrs. Winters dabbed her red-rimmed eyes with the shredded tissue. "Really?"

"Really. The fact that he's been talking a blue streak means that he probably didn't suffer any brain damage. He's alert and oriented and mad as hell. Which, for now, is just the way we like him."

Nora smiled reassuringly and received a wobbly one in return. "He does have a nasty bump on his head, but it doesn't seem to be bothering him and in a few days he'll probably be the star of his preschool.

"While we're waiting for your son to return from X ray, I'd like to get a bit more information. Why don't we go to my office?" she suggested. "The chairs are more comfortable than these hard plastic ones. And we'll have privacy."

The mother, appearing somewhat mollified, followed Nora meekly down the hallway.

Rather than place herself in the power spot behind her desk, Nora sat down on the suede chair adjacent to the matching sofa. "Does Jason have a regular pediatrician?"

"Yes." Mrs. Winters perched nervously on the edge of the sofa, looking prepared to bolt at any second. "Dr. Kline. His office is on Pine Street, but I can't remember the address." The tissue all but disintegrated, she began worrying the clasp of her brown suede purse with her fingers.

"No problem. We can look it up." Nora dutifully noted the information on the chart. "Is he currently taking any medication?"

"No." The purse popped open; Mrs. Winters absentmindedly snapped it shut again. As Nora questioned her about Jason's medical history, her fingers kept snapping and unsnapping, snapping and unsnapping.

Someone knocked on the door, then pushed it open. "Mr. Winters is here," Mabel informed Nora.

At that announcement, Mrs. Winters jumped. The opened purse slid off her lap; its contents scattered over the floor. The woman dropped to her knees and began frantically scooping up the collection of coins, grocery-store coupons and other items.

A man wearing the dark blue uniform of a police officer and the flushed look of a man terrified, but unable to admit it, entered the office.

"What happened?" he demanded of Nora, who noticed that he hadn't even bothered to glance at his wife. "Where's my son?"

"Your son fell out of his bedroom window. He's downstairs getting X rays," Nora said. She held out her hand. "I'm Dr. Nora Anderson, Jason's admitting physician.

"As I was telling your wife, Jason's injuries appear to be amazingly minor, but I ordered a CAT scan to make certain that he doesn't have internal injuries my examination failed to detect."

"He fell out the window?" He turned and looked down at his wife, who'd gone the color of library paste. "The window?" Furious red spots stained his weather-roughened cheeks. "How the hell did you let that happen?"

Their eyes locked. Nora couldn't detect a hint of compassion in either gaze.

"I've been begging you to put some kind of lock on that window for weeks," Mrs. Winters said, pushing herself to her feet with more energy than she'd displayed thus far. "But you're always too busy to help around the house."

"If I'm busy it's because I'm trying to keep a roof over our heads. You think I like working two jobs so you can quit work to stay home and neglect our kid?"

Her expression turned as hostile as her husband's. "I wasn't neglecting him! I was taking a shower. If you'd only gotten around to fixing that window—"

"If you were doing your damn job—"

Nora decided the time had come to intervene. "Mrs. Winters. Officer Winters. Please, sit down. I think we need to talk about your son. And what we all can do to help him recover."

That, apparently, was the magic word. The boy's parents exchanged a long look, then in unison, they sat down, each claiming a separate corner of the couch.

"Thank you." Nora took her own seat behind the desk and folded her hands atop the clipboard. "As I said, I don't believe Jason's injuries are going to turn out to be very severe. He is obviously a very lucky boy. Not only because it looks as if he's going to survive what could have been a fatal fall, but because he has two parents who care for him—deeply."

Mr. and Mrs. Winters nodded. "I do," they said together. It was Nora's turn to nod. "Good. Now, even if he escapes this with nothing more than a lump on his head, the entire experience, which would be frightening for you or me, is bound to be terrifying for a four-year-old child.

"And even if the CAT scan shows no further injuries, I'll want Jason to stay here for observation, which means that he'll be spending the night in a strange place.

"That being the case, your son will need your reassurance and support. He also needs to know that you don't blame him for his accident. If there's tension between you, he's liable to think that it's his fault."

She paused, allowing her words to sink in. "Believe me," she said quietly, "I understand how you're feeling."

Officer Winters shot her a withering look. "Don't patronize us, Dr. Anderson. No one knows what I'm feeling."

"I do," Nora argued. "Because I've been in your shoes."

She had never told the story to anyone before, and was shocked to hear the words coming from her lips. As she viewed their startled expressions, Nora decided that having finally captured their attention, she might as well continue.

"I'm ashamed to say that I reacted with emotion rather than logic, which only succeeded in making an already horrific situation even worse," she admitted, remembering how she'd railed at Caine and blamed him for the accident that had caused their son's death.

At the time, Caine hadn't even tried to defend himself.

And later, when she'd learned that the driver of the other car had been drunk and had crossed the centerline without giving Caine time to respond, she'd been too deeply immersed in her own pain to apologize.

"So," she said, "I would suggest that whatever your problems are, you manage to put them aside for now. For Jason's sake."

She paused again. The couple exchanged another long glance. "If you can't do that," Nora said quietly but firmly, "I'm going to have to ask that you visit your son separately."

Jason's father was looking down at the floor. His mother was dabbing ineffectually at her tears with the shredded, useless tissue. When the patrolman reached into a trouser pocket, took out a wide white handkerchief and began wiping at the moisture streaming down his wife's cheeks, Nora knew they'd made their decision.

She was also relieved when, caught up in their concern for their son, neither thought to ask her what the outcome of her own situation had been. Because as heartbreaking as Dylan's death had been, the still-vivid memory of how coldly she'd treated Caine, who'd been hurting himself, left Nora feeling confused. And guilty.

WHILE NORA STRUGGLED to sort out old and painful feelings, the object of all her discomfort was sitting at a table in a weather-beaten shack on the windswept Washington coast. In contrast to the sun that had been shining in Tribulation, the sky was low and gray, the rain streaking down the window matching Caine's gloomy mood.

The bar had been dubbed The No Name by locals after the sign had blown away during a typhoon more than two decades ago. The scent of cigarette smoke, spilled beer and mildew hung over the room like an oppressive cloud.

A lone woman, wearing a rhinestone-studded T-shirt, a skin-tight denim miniskirt and black, over-the-knee suede boots, put some coins in the jukebox and pressed B7.

As Garth Brooks began singing about the damn old rodeo, the woman sauntered over to Caine's table. "Hiya, handsome. How about a little Texas two-step?" she asked, swaying enticingly to the beat.

Caine signaled the bartender for another beer. "Sorry, sweetheart, but I'm just not in the mood for dancing today."

He nodded his thanks to the bartender who placed another can of Rainier on the table without stopping to take away the empties. The overflowing ashtray also went untended. "Maybe some other time."

"That's okay. I can think of lots better things to do on a rainy afternoon." She gave him a bold, suggestive smile. "My name's Micki. What's yours?"

"Caine." He lit another cigarette and blew out a stream of blue smoke.

"I've always liked biblical names." She sat down and crossed her long legs. "You know, Caine—" she leaned forward and placed her hand on his thigh "—perhaps if you stopped brooding over whoever or whatever it is that put that scowl on your face, you might find that you could have some fun, after all."

She had hit just a little too close to home for comfort. "You know, Micki, you may be on to something."

Caine tossed back the rest of the beer, ground the cigarette under the heel of his boot, tossed some bills on the table and with his arm around the woman's waist, walked out of the dark bar into the slanting silver rain.

A motel was conveniently located across the gravel

parking lot. Caine wasn't particularly surprised when the manager greeted the woman like an old friend. Neither was he surprised by the lecherous wink the guy gave him.

They'd no sooner entered the room when she turned, twined her bare arms around his neck and kissed him. As she pressed her mouth against his, Caine waited, with a certain fatalistic curiosity, for his body to respond. He wanted to see if this woman's scarlet lips could make him forget himself.

They couldn't.

Undeterred by his lack of response, Micki plopped down on the water bed, creating a series of waves. Outside the window, a steady stream of logging trucks passed, hissing wetly down the highway.

"You know, Caine, I knew the minute you walked into The No Name that you were the kind of guy who knew how to have a good time," she said, unzipping her high-heeled suede boots.

She and Caine had gotten soaked in their dash across the parking lot and the T-shirt clung to her like a second skin. Shivering, she tugged it over her head. Her bra was black and sheer, revealing nipples that had pebbled from the chill. For some inexplicable reason, Caine found himself comparing that overtly sexy bra with a utilitarian white maternity one he remembered Nora wearing. Irritated that the seemingly safe memory made him hard, he lipped a cigarette from the pack he'd managed to keep dry.

"Those things'll kill you," Micki said with a friendly smile.

Caine shrugged. "We all gotta go some time." He lighted the cigarette and inhaled the acrid smoke into his lungs.

"True enough."

She was down to a pair of black bikini panties. Rising from the bed, she walked over to the window, drew the smoke-stained orange drapes, then stopped in front of him. Plucking the cigarette from his lips, she took a long drag.

"But why do you want to waste time smoking when we could be setting that water bed on fire?"

Telling himself it was what he wanted, Caine jabbed the cigarette out in a nearby ceramic ashtray shaped like a fish and pulled her down onto the mattress, creating another wild tidal wave.

Micki was eager and talented, and everything a man could want in a bed partner.

So why the hell did his mutinous body betray him?

Caine's erection had softened like a deflated balloon and no amount of feminine coaxing could achieve success.

"That's okay," she assured him with what Caine considered inordinately good cheer a long time later. "It happens to everyone."

"Not to me." Frustrated, Caine muttered a low pungent curse.

He told himself that it was the depressing diagnosis he'd received from that Seattle doctor Nora had referred him to that had him in such a funk. Or the fact that the baseball season was in full swing without him on the mound. The beer he'd drunk, perhaps. Or the dreary weather.

Even as he made his way through the litany of possible excuses, Caine had a nagging feeling that the reason for his uncharacteristic inability to perform was that the woman stretched out so invitingly beside him on the water bed wasn't his ex-wife.

What the hell was Nora doing to his mind?

6

FOR MORE THAN A WEEK, Caine had avoided his family. Since he'd always thought of himself as the O'Halloran success story, the idea of returning home as a failure was anything but appealing.

Finally, however, knowing it was time—past time—to face them, he drove to his parents' house. He was almost relieved that no one was home. His next stop—the one he dreaded most—was his grandparents' home.

The old clapboard house was unchanged. The siding was still the faded grayish blue of a February sky, the porch railing as white as the snow that remained in patches beneath the dark green conifers surrounding the house.

Caine's grandfather, clad in a pair of dark blue overalls, a blue-and-black plaid shirt, a blue down-filled vest and a black watch cap, was sitting in a rocker on the porch, a pipestem jammed into the corner of his mouth.

Appearing unsurprised by the sight of a sleek black sports car pulling up in front of his home, he pushed himself out of the chair and came to stand by the railing.

Caine cut the engine and gazed through the tinted windows at his grandfather. When he was a boy, Caine had considered his grandfather the biggest, strongest man in the world. Even Paul Bunyan couldn't have whipped his "Pap," Caine remembered thinking.

He remembered this man's shoulders as being as

straight and wide as an ax handle. And the sure, majestic way Devlin O'Halloran moved had reminded Caine of a ship coming into harbor.

But now, taking in his grandfather's stooped shoulders, Caine was forced, once again, to realize that the world hadn't stopped turning just because Caine O'Halloran had gone away.

Taking a deep breath, he pushed the door open and climbed out of the low-slung car.

"Hi, Pappy." Caine stood at the bottom of the porch steps.

"'Bout time you decided to pay your old Pap a visit," the deep, wonderfully familiar voice growled. "I was beginnin' to think I was gonna have to keel over to get you to come home."

When Caine was five years old, he'd run to his grandfather, seeking sanctuary after breaking Mrs. Nelson's front window with a ball that had gone higher and farther than any ball he'd ever hit before.

As he climbed the front steps on this spring morning, he breathed in the familiar scents of Old Spice after-shave, cherry tobacco, hair tonic and the distant whiff of camphor his grandmother used to prevent moths from eating holes in her husband's beloved wool shirts, and realized that once again, he'd come to his grandfather seeking refuge.

"We heard you were back," Devlin O'Halloran said. "Looks like the rumor mill was well greased this time. That car does kinda remind me of a Batmobile."

Devlin's broad hands—hands capable of the delicate task of tying a fly to the end of a fishing line—took hold of Caine's arms as he gave him a long look.

"Also heard them Olson boys made mincemeat of your face." His still-bright blue eyes searched Caine's features.

"Your grandmother'll be happy to see that you don't look near as bad as folks are sayin'."

"Bruises fade."

"That they do," Devlin agreed. "So, how'd she look to you?"

"Who?"

"Don't play dumb with me, boy. I was talking about your wife, the doctor."

"She's my ex-wife."

"Bull." Devlin brushed Caine's words away as if they were a pesky fly. "Unless the Pope's gone on the television this morning and changed the rules while I've been sittin' here whittlin', the Church still doesn't cotton to divorce. So, the way I see it, the woman's still your wife."

"The way the state of New York sees it, Tiffany's my wife."

"From what I hear, not for long."

Although he'd yet to find anything humorous in his second wife's defection, Caine threw back his head, looked up at the bright blue sky and laughed. "News travels fast."

"Always has, around here," the older man agreed laconically. "And I'm sorry about you and that redheaded model, but I reckon that's what you get for marryin' a woman named after a jewelry store."

"I reckon you're right, Pappy."

His grandfather had always been able to coax a smile from him, even when things looked darkest. Nearly always, Caine corrected, remembering a time when even this man hadn't been able to lift the black cloud that had settled over him like a shroud.

"Heard you were out to the cemetery. Matty Johnson was raking the leaves off his wife's restin' place when he saw you puttin' flowers on Dylan's grave. Said he was gettin' ready to go over and welcome you back to town, when Nora showed up."

There was a question in the old man's voice that Caine knew he could not ignore. "We hadn't planned to meet. I guess my showing up unexpectedly triggered some old memories for her."

"That's what your grandmother and I figured. So?"

"So, what?"

"So, you two gonna be seein' each other regular?"

"It's a small town. We're bound to run into each other. And I've got an appointment to have some stitches taken out."

"Let me see."

Caine bent his head.

"She did a right fine job," Devlin allowed with surprise. "I remember your mother trying to teach that girl how to quilt. Finally gave up when she kept stitchin' her finger and bleedin' all over the squares."

"I guess she got better."

"Seems she did," Devlin agreed. "You eat breakfast?"

"Not yet. I figured I'd stop by the Timberline for coffee and one of Ingrid's Viking omelets after visiting you and Gram."

"And break your grandmother's heart? She made flapjack batter this morning and there's a jar of rhubarb sauce waitin' on the table with your name on it."

Caine grinned. His grandfather might look older, but some things, blessedly, remained the same. "Suddenly, I'm starving."

Devlin put his arm around Caine's shoulder and ushered him through the screen door into the kitchen.

"Your grandmother must be taking a nap," Devlin said.

"So early?" Caine glanced up at the copper teakettle clock over the stove. "It's only eight o'clock."

"She was up early. Pour yourself a cup of coffee and pull up a chair, Caine. I'll go check on her."

Devlin was smiling, but Caine heard concern in his grandfather's voice. "Is everything okay?"

"Just dandy." For the first time Caine could remember, his grandfather refused to look him in the eye. "Sit yourself down. I'll be back in two shakes of a lamb's tail."

Caine poured a cup of coffee from the dented aluminum coffeepot on the stove and took a careful sip. It was hot and dark and strong with a just a hint of chicory that hearkened back to Maggie O'Halloran's New Orleans roots.

The table was covered with the oilcloth that dated back to a time before Caine was born. The kitchen radio—an ancient tube model—was tuned to a big-band station, adding to the feeling that his grandparents' house had been frozen in time.

"She just drifted off," Devlin said, returning just as the Chattanooga choo-choo left Pennsylvania station. "I didn't think you'd want me to wake her."

"Of course not. Are you sure nothing's wrong?"

"Your grandmother's not a young woman, Caine. She gets a mite more tired these days. Same as the rest of us old codgers."

"Maybe I'd better have those flapjacks some other time."

"Don't be ridiculous," Devlin argued. "You stay put and I'll rustle them up before you can say Jack Sprat."

He moved toward the stove with the deliberate shuffle of a man of enormous energy trapped in an aging, stiff body. Caine wasn't about to sit by while a man nearly three times his age waited on him.

"How about we team up?"

"I reckon that'll be okay," Devlin replied. "But don't

you dare tell your grandmother. She'd have my hide if she found out I put you to work the minute you walked in the door."

"Mum's the word," Caine agreed.

They worked in companionable silence. Caine cooked the pancakes in an iron skillet in the center of the wood stove Maggie insisted cooked better than any gas or electric one, while Devlin fried bacon in the electric frying pan.

In the background, Glenn Miller was "in the mood," followed by Erskine Hawkins swinging in the Savoy Ballroom with "Tuxedo Junction." The batter began bubbling around the edges of the silver-dollar-size cakes.

"So what're you gonna do about getting Nora back?"

"What makes you think I want her back?" Caine flipped the pancakes.

"If you don't, you're a damn fool."

"Still beating around the bush, aren't you?"

"In case you hadn't noticed, boy, I'm gettin' to be an old man. The way I figure it, I don't have time to be subtle."

The pancakes were a golden brown. Caine piled them on a plate, put the plate in the warming oven, and began spooning more batter into the pan.

"I've got too much to work out without trying to rekindle cold ashes from a failed marriage," Caine muttered. Having his grandfather bring up his love life reminded him all too vividly of the other night's humiliating sexual failure.

The old man piled the bacon onto a platter, then shuffled over to the table and placed it in the middle of the oilcloth.

"You and Nora started out kinda rocky," Devlin allowed.

Caine watched him struggling with the lid of the preserve jar and had to force himself not to rush in to help. "We ended that way, too," Caine reminded him.

Devlin shrugged. "Every marriage goes through a few rough patches. You gonna turn those or let 'em burn?"

Caine flipped the round cakes just in time.

He was relieved when his grandfather appeared willing to drop the subject while they shared a companionable breakfast.

"It's good to have you back, Caine," Devlin said, spooning the dark red rhubarb sauce over their pancakes.

"You've no idea how good it is to *be* back." Caine took a bite and remembered what heaven tasted like.

"There's been a lot of changes here on the peninsula," Devlin complained. "We're gettin' more overrun with tourists every day...the kind of folks that look like they just stepped off the pages of one of them L. L. Bean or Eddie Bauer catalogs.

"Used to be you could leave your tackle in your boat—can't do that anymore. Remember the first time I took you fishing?"

"We were out for seven days, trolling for salmon."

He'd been five at the time, but Caine could remember the cold winds, the churning waves and the orange floats as if it were yesterday. The memory was so vivid that when he took a bite of bacon, Caine was almost surprised that it didn't taste of fish.

"I was as sick as a dog the entire time."

"You were a mite green around the gills," Devlin confirmed. "I told your daddy that we'd better find you another occupation because it was obvious that you weren't born with the O'Halloran sea legs. Next day he bought you your first baseball."

He stabbed a piece of pancake with his fork and chewed thoughtfully. "Funny how things work out. Who would've guessed that you'd grow up to be a big-league baseball star and end up in the Hall of Fame alongside Ruth and DiMaggio and Cobb?"

"You can't get voted into the Hall of Fame until you've been retired for five years. And I'm not ready to retire."

"Your daddy said the same thing," Devlin observed. "What with all the government quotas, a string of bad weather, and foreigners working the waters, the fishing business has gotten so bad it looks like your daddy might have to give up *The Bountiful*."

"I went by the docks to see *The Bountiful* yesterday," Caine told him. He'd been surprised by the number of streamlined sport-fishing craft, painted red and blue and yellow, with sickeningly cute names and long whip antennae, that had taken over many of the old fishing-boat slips. "But they told me she was out to sea."

"Your daddy got himself a two-week charter. A bunch of insurance guys from Seattle won some kinda sales contest.

"That's one of those funny twists of fate. For a while, things were lookin' so bad we thought your daddy would have to turn *The Bountiful* over to the bank and go work on the beach."

"I hadn't realized he was in financial trouble. Damn! Why didn't he tell me?"

"It wasn't your problem."

"But I made three million dollars last year."

Devlin looked up with interest. "Newspapers said four point five."

"The newspapers were wrong."

"Still," Devlin mulled aloud, "three million is a right nice piece of change."

"Enough to pay every debt my father could have racked up and buy a fleet of new boats." Caine's fingers curved tightly around the handle of his fork. "Dammit, he should have told me."

"You had your own troubles, what with your injury and your marriage problems and all," his grandfather argued patiently. "We didn't want to worry you."

Although Devlin didn't say it, Caine had the bleak feeling that the reason his family hadn't come to him for help was that they'd never considered him all that reliable. Although he knew his parents were proud of his achievements, he also knew that they found it difficult to view baseball as a real job.

The O'Hallorans were a hardy, unpretentious, salt-of-the-earth breed who'd always worked hard for every penny; he, on the other hand, was paid a virtual fortune to play a kids' game. Add to that a press corps that loved detailing his admittedly hedonistic life-style, and it was no wonder his parents had opted to handle their own financial problems.

Caine shrugged. "I had a few curveballs thrown my way. Nothing I can't handle. Dad should have said something."

"'Tweren't necessary. A few months ago your daddy turned the boat into a charter and Ellen signed on as cook. Thanks to city slickers with too much time and money on their hands, he's makin' more in a month than he did all last year. Which leads me to my next point."

"What point is that?" Caine knew he sounded like a petulant twelve-year-old. Which wasn't surprising since, unfortunately, at the moment he felt like one.

"That sometimes life takes funny turns and it looks as if things are goin' downhill, but if a fella's quick on the uptake, he can turn things around to his advantage.

"Nothin' your daddy liked better than bein' out on that boat. And for a while, it looked like he was gonna have to give it up. But then he figured out this charter business and from what I can tell he's never been happier.

"And your mama. Lord, that lady never worked for wages a day in her life, but you'd think she'd discovered heaven from the way she talks about all the pleasure she gets from those city folk gobblin' up her vittles like they'd been starving.

"So, why don't you quit feelin' sorry for yourself, Caine, and figure out how to make lemonade outta them lemons fate dealt you?"

Caine squared his shoulders. "I'm not feeling sorry for myself."

"Who's not feelin' sorry for himself?" a feminine voice asked. "Is that my Caine?" Maggie O'Halloran peered through her wire-framed glasses as she entered the kitchen.

She was wearing a scarlet sweatshirt embossed with a trio of puffins sitting atop a rock and blue jeans that hung loosely, suggesting that she'd lost a great deal of weight recently. Her hair, once a flaming red, had faded to a soft tapestry of silver-and-pink.

"Hiya, Gram."

Caine pushed himself out of his chair, crossed the room and enfolded her in his arms. She was smaller than he remembered—the top of her head barely reached the middle of his chest—and she seemed unusually frail.

"God, it's good to see you."

She tilted her head back. "Still using the Lord's name in vain, I see." There was a twinkle in her blue eyes. "What on earth are we gonna do with you, Caine O'Halloran?"

"There's always the woodshed."

She chuckled at that. "You were too big for a whupping when you were born. Guess I'll have to give you a big hug instead."

As she wrapped her arms around him, Caine couldn't help noticing that her strength wasn't what it once had been. He drank in the familiar scent of lilacs that had always surrounded her and tried to pretend that nothing had changed.

"You're sure looking good, Gram," he said. He grinned at his grandfather over the top of her pastel curls. "You'd better watch out, Pappy, or one of those big Swede loggers is gonna steal this lady right out from under your nose."

"Lars Nelson winked at her last Friday," Devlin allowed.

"That wasn't a wink," Maggie argued. "The old man just has a tic in his left eye."

"Sure looked like a wink to me," Devlin said. "I thought maybe he was lookin' for a refresher course on those flying lessons he took from you."

"That was fifty years ago," Maggie informed Caine. "And your grandfather's still jealous."

The three of them laughed at the long-running joke.

"Besides," Maggie said as she made her way slowly and painfully, Caine noticed with alarm, to a chair, "I haven't been up in a plane for so long I probably couldn't remember how to take off."

"I doubt that, Gram," Caine said. "Everyone knows you were born to fly."

"You're right about that," Maggie agreed, smiling her thanks to her husband, who'd placed a mug of coffee liberally laced with milk in front of her. "Of course I had a heck of a time convincing others of that fact, back in the old days."

She blew on the coffee, took a sip, then gazed down into the light brown depths as if seeing herself as she'd been in those days so many years ago. As if on cue, Les Brown's "Sentimental Journey" came over the radio.

"They wouldn't let me solo, so I couldn't get my license."

Caine knew the romantic story of his grandmother's life by rote. Maggie O'Halloran, nee Margaret Rose Murphy, had been born in New Orleans in 1910. When she was fifteen years old, she'd run away from the convent school her wealthy parents had sent her to and become a singer and dancer on the Orpheum circuit.

It was during her days on the stage that she'd met a dashing former World War I flying ace barnstorming his way across America. He'd taken her up in his Lockheed Vega and although the pilot had moved on the following morning, Maggie's love affair with the airplane had lasted the rest of her life.

Caine had heard innumerable stories of Maggie's exploits while growing up, including how Devlin, who loved the way Maggie Murphy looked in her scandalous khaki trousers, had vowed to win the heart of the hot-tempered, flame-haired aviatrix.

Noticing the familiar warm light shining in her eyes, Caine was more than willing to sit through the story again.

"But eventually you got it," he said, on cue.

"Sure did." She chuckled, then took another sip. "Of course, it was still a man's world, and I got turned down for every airline job I applied for, but then one day I showed up at this itsy-bitsy airfield in Glendale, California, where they were having a pylon race. Won myself a trophy, which I ended up pawning to pay for fuel for my next three races."

A reminiscent smile wreathed her face, softening the lines earned from a lifetime of working outdoors. "Boy, I loved beating those egotistical swaggering pilots with their goggles and their flowing white silk scarves. Why, by the time Amelia Earhart handed me that cross-country trophy in 1937, I had more flying hours than she did."

"Looked better in trousers, too," Devlin drawled.

"And you were always a silver-tongued devil, Devlin O'Halloran." A soft flush colored her cheeks, and Caine experienced a twinge of envy at this couple who, after more than fifty years of marriage, were still so much in love.

He was still considering exactly how they'd managed such a remarkable feat when his grandmother's head dropped to her chest.

"Gram?" He was on his feet and around the table like a shot.

"She's been droppin' off like that regular," his grandfather assured him. "Nora says it's normal."

"But she just woke up."

"And now she's sleepin'. Let it be, Caine."

But he couldn't. There was something wrong with Maggie. Something his grandfather wasn't saying. And if Devlin wasn't going to tell him the truth about his grandmother's condition, he had no choice but to get it from Nora.

"Thanks for the breakfast," he said. "I'll do the dishes."

"No need to worry about them. I'll stick them in the dishwasher." Devlin gave Caine a warning look. "Maggie wouldn't want you goin' off half-cocked, making a fuss about her."

"But she's sick."

"She's old," his grandfather corrected. "Let it be, Caine," he said again.

Caine shrugged. "Sure, whatever you say."

They both knew it was a lie.

Caine gave his grandfather a farewell hug and walked back out to the car, feeling as if the entire weight of the world was lying heavily on his shoulders.

JOHNNY BAKER WAS SEVEN years old. His uncombed hair was the color of butterscotch candy, his bare feet were dirty and his eyes were older and more resigned than any seven-year-old's eyes had a right to be.

In a way, Johnny was lucky. His burns, which his mother alleged he'd received when he'd accidentally overturned a pot of boiling water, were no worse than a medium-harsh sunburn. If the circumstances had been different, Nora would have sent him home with a tube of analgesic ointment.

But there was something about the burns themselves that bothered her. The skin on both too-thin reddened arms had clear demarcation lines; there were none of the splash marks she would have expected above the burned area.

And there were other faint scars, on the insides of the boy's arms and buttocks. Small, round, wrinkled white scars. Nora had seen marks like that before.

When the X rays showed what Nora had feared, she placed a call to Children's Protective Services and began filling out the admission form that would keep the little boy in the hospital until an investigation could be launched.

She'd just finished the paperwork when her office door opened. She glanced up, then had to fight the unbidden pleasure that surged through her when she saw Caine standing there.

"Hi." She started to rise, then changed her mind, not wanting to give up the three feet of polished desk between them. "This is a surprise."

"I need to talk to you."

"Oh, Caine. I told you—"

"It's not about us," he said quickly. "It's about Maggie."

"Oh." She folded her hands atop the manila file. "I take it you've seen her."

"This morning. And it's obvious that something's wrong with her, but my grandfather refuses to talk about it."

"I know." Nora sighed. "It's hard on him. The thought of losing her."

"My grandmother's dying?" She'd confirmed Caine's worst fears. Pain ripped through him, more brutal and severe than anything the Olson boys could have dished out.

"We're all dying, Caine," Nora reminded him quietly. "It's just that Maggie's time is getting close."

"What's wrong with her?"

She gestured toward a chair on the visitors' side of the desk. "Please, sit down. Would you like some coffee?"

"This isn't a damn tea party, Nora," Caine growled. "You don't have to play hostess. I just want to know what's wrong with my grandmother."

"Other than old age?"

He snorted in a disbelieving way. "She's only eighty-two, dammit. Both her parents lived into their late nineties. We were talking and she fell asleep in the middle of a conversation. You can't tell me that's normal. Even at her age."

"No." His face was as dark and threatening as a thundercloud. Nora tried to decide where to begin. "A few years ago, Maggie was diagnosed as having sideroblastic anemia."

"I remember that. Mom wrote me about it. But she said

that so long as Gram received regular transfusions, she'd be fine."

"And she was. Until recently. Devlin came to me when I first opened my practice, worried because she kept falling asleep. He couldn't talk her into going to a doctor, so he wanted my help."

"Gram always did like you."

"I love her," Nora said simply. "The problem is, as you know, your grandmother's a fairly stubborn woman."

"That's putting it mildly. When Maggie Murphy O'Halloran digs in her heels, she can put a pit bull terrier to shame."

"Exactly. Finally, after a great deal of unprofessional pleading and cajoling, I managed to talk her into going to Seattle for some extensive tests."

"And?"

"She has hemochromatosis, Caine."

"What the hell is that?"

"The diagnosis is complex, but the gist of it is that the iron deposits from all the blood transfusions are keeping her heart from contracting effectively. Which is why she can't stay awake. Her heart can only pump effectively for a short time, then it has to rest."

"So get her a new heart."

"I wish it were that simple. But it's not."

"Sure, it is. I made three million dollars last year."

"The papers said four point five."

If he weren't so worried about Maggie, Caine would have found it interesting that Nora had bothered reading about him.

"They were wrong. It was three. But that's still six zeros, Nora. Surely that's enough to buy Gram a new heart."

"Even if you could just run to a body-parts store and

pick up a new heart, which you can't, a transplant is not an option in Maggie's case."

"Why not?"

"In the first place, Maggie isn't well enough to survive the wait for a donor heart, even if we could get her on the list.

"In the second place, if a heart did become available in time, I doubt she could survive the surgery."

"It's worth a try."

"Not to her."

"What?"

"Maggie categorically refuses to consider any dramatic efforts to keep her alive."

Caine ground his teeth so hard his jaw ached. "That's ridiculous."

"It's her decision. And," Nora added softly, "one Devlin and I happen to agree with."

His face took on that familiar, stubborn expression she knew all too well. His eyes turned to flint, his jaw jutted forward.

"Gram's always listened to me. I can change her mind."

"Caine, don't do this."

Nora rose from her chair and went around the desk to stand in front of him. "Maggie's made her decision. She's comfortable with it. Please don't upset her."

Caine was on his feet, as well. "I'm trying to save her life, dammit!"

"That's just the point." Nora put her hand on his arm and felt the muscle tense beneath her fingertips. "You can't save her, Caine. No one can."

Caine muttered a litany of harsh expletives. "I am not going to let her die."

Nora remembered the paramedics trying to tell her that

Caine had been shouting the same thing while the rescue team cut Dylan out of the mangled red Corvette.

"I'm sorry, Caine. Truly, I am."

"Goddamn it!" He pulled away from her and slammed his fist into the wall, punching a hole in the plasterboard. Unsatisfied, he gave the wall a vicious kick with the toe of his boot. The impact sent a jolt of lightning through his healing ribs.

"Are you all right?"

"I'm fine." He flexed his fingers. "See?" His tired gaze took in the ragged hole. "Send me the bill for your wall."

"Don't worry about it."

"I said, send me the damn bill."

"Fine, I'll send you the damn bill."

"Good." He nodded. "I'm going to get a second opinion."

"You have every right to do that," Nora told him. "But I have to warn you, Caine, all the specialists who saw Maggie agreed with the diagnosis. And she doesn't have the strength to have you dragging her all over the country."

"Shit." He threw his long frame onto the office sofa, put his head against the back cushion and covered his eyes with his hand. "Now what?"

"I suggested Maggie enter a hospice program so she can stay at home, instead of spending her last months in the hospital."

"She'd hate being stuck in some dreary hospital room," Caine said glumly. "So is she in this program?"

"She hasn't made up her mind yet. Perhaps you can help convince her."

Caine nodded. "I'll give it my best shot." He gave her a long, probing look. "What's the prognosis?"

"I told you—"

"I know." He cut the air with a swift slice of his hand. "You've convinced me that my grandmother is going to die, Nora. I want to know when. And how."

She'd seen that expression on his face before. When he'd been waiting for word of their critically injured son. Immersed in her own fear, Nora had refused to acknowledge his pain. This time, she found it impossible to ignore.

"It's hard to say," she said softly. "She could have a heart attack, or a stroke, or some other type of seizure. Or she might simply fall asleep one of these times and not wake up."

"Not a lot of nifty options, huh?"

"I'm sorry."

He looked at her, taking in her neat blond hair, her starched white jacket, the little rectangular name tag above her right breast. She seemed both familiar and foreign at the same time. Caine wondered if Nora realized that the severe tailoring of her professional clothing made her appear all the more feminine by contrast. Softer.

"I never could really think of you as a doctor."

"I know." It was one of the things they'd fought about on a regular basis.

"But you're pretty good. I'm impressed."

The faintest of smiles played at the corners of her full, serious mouth. "Thank you. I needed a kind word today."

He glanced over at the light box she'd left on. "Trouble with one of your patients?"

"A seven-year-old boy. His mother brought him in with burns she said he'd gotten from pulling a pan off the stove."

"I hope they're not too bad."

"Actually, they probably won't even blister. But I had a funny feeling about it, so I ordered some X rays."

"And?"

"See these?" Nora picked up a pencil and began pointing to various faint lines on the gray film.

Caine pushed himself off the couch and came over to stand beside her. "Those wiggly lines?"

"Those are old fractures left to heal by themselves."

"The kid was beaten?"

"Apparently. And there're more." Nora turned off the light. "There were scars about the size of a pencil eraser."

"Or a lighted cigarette." Caine felt suddenly sick.

"Or a lighted cigarette," Nora agreed flatly.

Caine wondered how it was that he and Nora, who'd loved Dylan so much, had lost him, while some other parents could deliberately hurt their child.

"Makes you wonder, doesn't it?"

She looked up into his face and read her own troubled thoughts in his pained gaze. "Yes." Her voice came out in a whisper. "It does."

They stood there, only inches apart, looking at each other, bittersweet memories swirling in the air between them.

"Nora." He ran his palm down the silk of her hair and watched the awareness rise in her eyes.

"Oh, Caine." It was little more than a whisper.

He leaned closer.

"This is a mistake," she warned.

"Probably. But no worse than any of the others I've been making lately." His knuckles caressed her cheek in a slow, seductive sweep. "And I'm willing to bet it'll be a helluva lot more enjoyable than most."

7

AS HIS LIPS TOUCHED hers, the intervening years spun away and all the reasons why this was a mistake dissolved like mist over the treetops.

Holding Nora brought not the pain of lost love he would have expected, but a rightness—almost a contentment—Caine hadn't expected to feel. How could he have forgotten how sweet she was? And how responsive.

He felt her sigh against his mouth—a slow, shuddering breath that echoed his own pleasure. Time tumbled backward, taking them past the pain to a passion that had been even more exquisite because it had been so liberally laced with love.

"God, I've missed this." Caine drew her closer, then closer still, until the rising heat threatened to fuse their bodies. "I've missed you." Although he'd never realized it, it was true.

"Don't talk," she whispered breathlessly. "Just kiss me. And hold me." Her arms wrapped possessively around him; her lips fused with his, again and again. "Tight."

Dear Lord, he was lost in her. In her touch, her taste, her scent. Nora was everything he'd been wanting, without even knowing he'd been wanting it. She was everything he'd been needing without knowing he'd been needing it. She was heaven.

She was home.

Home. The word, which once had represented unwanted strings and unwelcome commitments, now seemed like a prayer.

Caine skimmed his lips along the line of her jaw, then up her cheek to linger at her temple. Desperate to know how her body had changed during their years apart, he slipped his hands inside her lab coat. When his wide hand cupped her breast, a ragged moan escaped her parted lips.

He tugged her blouse loose, then her camisole, inching his way beneath the ivory silk. "You feel so good."

His fingers moved upward to stroke her breasts, finding them as smooth and firm and fragrant as he remembered.

He wanted to take those taut peaks in his mouth. He wanted to feel her body, hot and eager and open against his. He wanted to possess her, mind and body and soul, as he'd done on so many nights so long ago.

He was actually considering the logistics of making love to her here and now in her office, when her intercom buzzed sharply.

Like a man immersed in a sensual dream, Caine was aware of the intrusion and fought against it.

The intercom continued to buzz.

"I have to answer that." Her flat tone told him it was not her first choice.

Without removing his hands from beneath her camisole, he tugged her pearl earring off with his teeth and dropped it onto the desk before nibbling at her earlobe. "Don't tell me this hospital will come to a halt if you don't answer your intercom?"

"No, but the ER clerk has a habit of just barging in."

Knowing that the idea of being caught in a heated clench with her ex-husband was more than Nora could handle, Caine reluctantly released her, then reached out to steady her when she suddenly swayed.

"You okay?"

"Of course." But her hand trembled as she finger-combed her sleek hair.

"Remind me to stop by Richie Duggan's hardware store and get a Do Not Disturb sign for your office door."

"Please, Caine." She struggled to tuck her blouse back into her waistband. "Don't do this."

They were on familiar turf again: Nora backing away, Caine pressing her for more than she wanted to give.

"I didn't do it alone."

"I know." Her eyes, her voice, revealed her regret.

There was a sharp knock on the door. A moment later, Mabel entered the office.

"Is everything all right, Dr. Anderson?"

The elderly woman's gaze reminded Caine of a curious bird's as it flicked from Nora to him and back to Nora.

"Everything's fine," Nora answered in a tone that was not nearly as strong as her usual professional voice.

"You sure?" Knowing eyes searched Nora's flushed face.

"Of course."

"You didn't answer the intercom."

"Mr. O'Halloran and I were discussing his grand-mother's case," Nora said.

Mabel turned back toward Caine, who was standing with his arms crossed over his broad chest. "I thought I recognized you."

"Mabel Erickson, Caine O'Halloran," Nora introduced them reluctantly. "Mabel runs the emergency room."

"No wonder everyone looks so efficient," Caine said. "Believe me, Ms. Erickson, I've been in a lot of emergency rooms over the years and I could tell right away that yours is one of the best."

"Call me Mabel." She beamed. "I've got your *Playgirl* calendar in my locker," she surprised Nora by revealing. "If I go get it, will you autograph it for me?"

Caine grinned. "I'll stop by your desk on my way out."

Mabel's fleshy, smiling face was the hue of a late-July raspberry. "Don't you dare leave this hospital without signing it."

"I wouldn't think of it," Caine said easily.

"Mabel?" Nora called out to the receptionist's back.

The clerk stopped on her way out the door and glanced back over her shoulder. "Yes, Dr. Anderson?"

"What did you want?"

"Want?" Mabel's gaze slid back to Caine.

"The intercom," Nora reminded her. "You buzzed."

"Oh, that. The Protective Service's social worker is here. About that little boy. I put her in waiting room B."

"Thank you." But Mabel had already bustled off toward the staff locker room, leaving Nora talking to air.

"You've obviously made another conquest," she snapped.

Her withdrawal was as familiar as her smoldering sexuality. Caine remembered all too well how Nora had never grown accustomed to having her husband surrounded by baseball groupies. Not that she'd ever needed to worry.

Recalling her passion that Midsummer Eve in the cabin, Caine hadn't been terribly surprised when their first encounter as man and wife six months after their marriage confirmed his long-held belief that they were a perfect sexual match.

What had come as a distinct shock that afternoon years ago, before their son was born, was the realization that somehow, when he wasn't looking, he'd fallen head over heels in love with his wife.

"I don't think this is the time or the place to get into another argument about my alleged infidelities, Nora," Caine said now. His mouth set in its grim line again; all the heated emotion he'd displayed in his kiss had disappeared from his eyes.

"It's a moot point," Nora said between clenched teeth, "since it's over between us. I gave up worrying about all your other women a very long time ago, Caine."

She brushed her hands down the front of her jacket, smoothing the wrinkles that remained as damning evidence of her uncharacteristically unprofessional behavior.

Caine rubbed his jaw. "You know, I thought it was over, too. But I'm beginning to have my doubts."

She tilted her chin. "I haven't any doubts."

"Not even one?"

"None at all."

He could have murdered her for unleashing so much raw emotion, then behaving as if that shared kiss had never happened. He could have dragged her onto the couch, her desk, hell, the floor, to prove to her how very wrong she was.

"Well, then, if that's really the case, we shouldn't have any problem getting along while you're treating Maggie."

Maggie. Caine couldn't accept the idea that his grandmother was dying. It was something he would have to think about later. When he was alone. Or better yet, with his new best friend, Jack Daniel's.

"No problem at all," Nora agreed stiffly. "I really do have to leave." Unwilling to look directly at him, Nora focused on the wall thermostat beside the door.

"Before you go, can I ask what happens next?"

"With us? I told you, Caine. Nothing."

Caine saw the lingering reluctant desire she hadn't been able to hide glowing in her eyes. That she wanted him was obvious. That she didn't want to want him was also all too apparent.

It was just as well, he decided grimly. He had enough problems right now without getting involved with the only woman he'd ever met who could make him willing to beg.

"Actually, I was referring to that little boy."

"Oh." Embarrassed that she'd misunderstood him and surprised by his obvious concern for someone other than himself, she said, "Children's Protective Services will begin an investigation. I could release him this afternoon, but I'd rather keep him here and avoid the risk of the social workers deciding to leave him with his mother while they conduct the investigation."

"Can you do that?" Caine asked. Concern for the unfortunate child temporarily overrode his concern for Maggie. "When there really isn't anything wrong with him?"

"You can always find something wrong with a kid if you're creative."

"Sounds as if you've had some experience with this."

"More than I'd like." She picked up the file, prepared to leave the office. "I really do have to leave."

"Sure." Caine stepped aside. "Do you think it'd be okay if I dropped in on the kid?"

"That would be terrific. I don't know why I didn't think of it myself." She rewarded him with a faint, appreciative smile. "He's upstairs on the pediatric ward. Perhaps you could go up now while I talk with the social worker."

"Great." He frowned. "I just wish I had a baseball or something for him."

"I think meeting you will be tonic enough." The smile

reached her eyes as she put her hand on his arm. "Thank you."

"No thanks necessary, Doc." Caine covered her hand with his own. "I'm just happy to be able to help out."

He decided, for discretion's sake, not to admit that if he were to go home to that lonely cabin to think about Maggie, and face his undeniable role in the failure of his and Nora's marriage, he'd give in to the need to get very very drunk.

Her soft smile—a portent that perhaps things might be looking up—stayed with Caine as he took the elevator to the second-floor pediatric wing.

For a man who'd been seeking something—someone—to make him feel like a hero again, Johnny Baker proved the perfect prescription.

But it was more than just being put atop his lofty pedestal again, which, Caine considered, wasn't all that bad. After drowning in self-pity for months, one look at those small bandaged hands went a long way to putting things back into perspective. If what Nora suspected was true, fate had certainly dealt this kid more than his share of rotten luck.

Although Johnny had surrounded himself with protective walls even Nora might have envied, after a few minutes of regaling the seven-year-old with tales of games past, Caine began to breach those parapets.

Enough so that Johnny had actually begun to relax when Nora entered the room with the social worker.

"Look who came to see me, Dr. Anderson," Johnny greeted her. "Caine O'Halloran." He breathed the name in the way a religious zealot might whisper the name of his god. Johnny's eyes, which had been so flat and lifeless during her examination, gleamed with youthful enthusiasm.

"Dr. Anderson and I are old friends," Caine said.

"Wow!" The boy's gaze went back and forth between them. "You're really lucky, Dr. Anderson."

"I guess I am at that," Nora said.

"You know what?"

"What?"

"He's gonna bring me an autographed baseball."

"And a Yankees cap," Caine reminded him.

"Yeah." Johnny Baker's expression was that of a boy for whom Christmas had come seven months early. "A real Yankees cap. Autographed by Billy Martin and Mickey Mantle!"

Knowing how he had revered that particular piece of baseball memorabilia, Nora looked up at Caine in surprise and received an embarrassed grin in return.

"That's wonderful," she said with a smile. "Johnny, this is Mrs. Langley. She'd like to have a little chat with you."

The light left his eyes, like a candle snuffed out by an icy wind. "You're from Social Services, aren't you?" He said the words without emotion, but his flat, older-than-his-years tone touched Caine more deeply than his earlier hero worship.

A little pool of silence settled over the room. "Yes, I am," the social worker agreed quietly.

Thin shoulders, clad in a pair of the Superhero pajamas given to all the little boys on the ward, lifted and fell in a resigned shrug. "I figured you were."

"Have you talked with social workers before, Johnny?" Nora asked.

"Yeah. In Portland. And a couple times in L.A. And every time, Mama'd get mad afterward and we'd have to move again." He sighed. "I'm gettin' awful tired of moving."

"Perhaps you won't have to," Mrs. Langley suggested. She pulled a chair up to the side of the bed. When she sat down, she was at eye level with the boy. "Perhaps this time, things will be different."

He stiffened slightly, as if bracing for the worst. "That's what they all say."

He was retreating, back behind those self-protective walls. Feeling the boy's pain and experiencing a strange sort of kinship with this child whose life had started out on such a different path from his own, Caine squeezed Johnny's shoulder.

"Listen, sport. I've got a feeling that between the four of us in this room, we can make a difference. But you've got to help."

"How?" A glimmer of hope cut through the shadows as Johnny looked up at his hero.

"You've got to tell the truth." When the seven-year-old didn't immediately answer, Caine leaned closer and whispered in his ear.

"I'll think about it," Johnny replied. "But only if you promise."

"Scout's honor."

Johnny Baker looked into Caine's face for a long time. "I guess I can trust you."

"I wouldn't let you down, Johnny. You can count on it."

Apparently making his decision, the boy turned back to the social worker. "So, what do you want to know?"

"What did you say to make him change his mind?" Nora asked, as she and Caine left the room.

She'd seen similar cases where there were obvious signs of abuse and the children, whether from fear or misplaced loyalty, absolutely refused to say a single accusing word against their parents.

"Not that much." Caine pushed the elevator button. "I simply told him that I wouldn't let Social Services send him back to his mother."

"Caine!" Nora stared up at him. "You had no right to tell him any such thing!"

"Why not?"

"Because you have no control over the situation."

"Of course I do."

The elevator reached the floor; the green metal doors opened. Caine stood aside and gestured for Nora to enter first.

"If Social Services drops the ball and lets his mother take him back home again," Caine said as he followed her into the elevator and pushed the button for the first floor, "I'll call a press conference and tell everyone in the state what she's done. That should get the bureaucrats off their behinds."

"You can't do that!"

"Why not?"

"Because the mother could turn around and sue you for libel, or slander."

"Let her sue," Caine said. "I'll just hire the best attorney in the country and keep her tied up in court until the kid's an adult and safely out of her control."

He meant it, Nora realized, stunned by this man she'd thought she knew so well. "Why would you go out on a limb for a child you don't even know?"

"Why would you?" he countered. "Obviously filing a suspected abuse form is not something a doctor does without weighing all the options."

"He's a child at risk. I had no choice."

"Exactly." Caine nodded, satisfied. The car reached their floor. "And believe it or not, for once in our lives, we're in perfect agreement." He followed her out of the elevator. "And there's something else."

"What?"

"Dylan probably would have looked a lot like Johnny Baker," Caine said in a hushed, pained voice. "If he'd lived."

"Dammit, Caine..."

Tears began to well in Nora's eyes and she turned away. She felt his hand on her shoulder.

"Don't you think it's finally time we dealt with it, Nora?"

She could have wept with relief when the speaker above her head began to blare a code. "I've got to go," she said. "I'm on duty."

He dropped his hand to his side. "What time do you get off?"

"Three-thirty, but—"

"I'll be waiting."

"But, Caine..." The code continued to blare. "Oh, hell. Do whatever you want. You always have." Welcoming the irritation that steamrolled over her earlier emotional turmoil, she took off running to the ambulance entrance.

Caine watched her talking to the paramedics as they pulled a gurney from the back of the red-and-white vehicle. She was no longer the young woman he'd seduced in front of a crackling fire on Midsummer Eve so many years ago. Nor was she the exhausted, surprisingly insecure, angry bride he'd alternately fought with, shared terrific sex with, and ultimately abandoned.

A late bloomer, Dr. Nora Anderson had definitely come into her own. That she was satisfied—even happy—with her life was obvious.

Not for the first time since returning to Tribulation, Caine wished he could learn her secret.

NORA WAS NOT SURPRISED to find Caine waiting for her when she left the hospital that afternoon. Nor was she all that surprised that he'd ignored all the posted signs and parked in the staff parking lot.

"Eric was right," she said as she approached the man who was leaning against the gleaming black car. "That Ferrari does look like the Batmobile."

"I know." Caine grinned. "It's a ridiculously juvenile car for a grown man, but I couldn't help myself. Think I'm going through male menopause, Doc?"

Her mind, so calm and deliberate earlier in the emergency room, sprang to fevered life at his cocky grin. Her body followed at an alarming pace.

"That would be a little difficult," she said in a dry tone meant to conceal the havoc going on inside her, "since emotionally, you still haven't gotten out of your teens."

The smile in her eyes took the sting out of her words. "Ouch. You really know how to hurt a guy, don't you? And here I thought we were becoming friends."

"Fine. As your friend, I feel it's my duty to point out that you're parked in a reserved spot."

"It was empty."

"It belongs to the chief of staff."

"If the guy worked a full day like he was supposed to, his spot wouldn't have been vacant, so I couldn't have taken it," Caine argued. "So, what was your big emergency?"

"A sixteen-year-old girl was kicked in the abdomen by a horse."

"Is she going to be okay?"

"It's touch and go. The surgeon repaired her lacerated liver and removed a ruptured kidney, but it's still iffy." Nora frowned. "Here's a kid who could very well die and you know what she's worried about?"

"That her parents are going to get rid of her horse?"

"Exactly. How did you know?"

Caine shrugged. "You're the one who pointed out that I still haven't outgrown my teenage stage. I guess I can identify with a sixteen-year-old kid."

"I'm sorry about that. I was out of line. Especially after the way you jumped to Johnny Baker's defense." Nora managed a weak smile. "I suppose I could use the excuse that I'm exhausted, but I think the truth is that snapping at you is a leftover knee-jerk reaction."

"Makes sense to me," Caine said agreeably. "Since I'm suffering from a few old knee-jerk responses myself."

"Really?"

"Really. Except in my case, the feelings are a bit different."

Nora saw the devil in his eye and turned away to unlock her car door.

"Don't you want to know what they are?"

"Not really," she said with pretended indifference, struggling to turn a key in the lock.

"I think I'll tell you anyway." He plucked the keys from her hand, located the correct one and unlocked the door. "I can't seem to resist the urge to taste you whenever those ridiculously kissable lips come within puckering distance.

Before she could get into the car, he cupped her chin, lifted her frowning lips to his and gave her a long, deep kiss that left them both breathless.

"We still set off sparks, Nora," he murmured when they finally came up for air.

He brushed the pad of his ultrasensitized thumb against the flesh of her bottom lip. Caine's heart was pounding with a rhythm he usually associated with spring-training wind sprints. He'd never met another woman who could make him suffer so, and relish the pain.

"You can't deny it, babe."

"It's only sex. Nothing more."

"You were always good for my ego."

"And you always had sex on the brain."

Amusement flickered in his eyes as he skimmed a slow, sensual glance over her. "I don't remember you complaining."

Once again the atmosphere between them had become intensely charged. "Dammit, Caine—"

"Besides," he said, "I think we were wrong."

"About what?"

"About the only thing we had going for us in those days, besides Dylan, was sex. Oh, I know that's what we always used to say," he said when she opened her mouth to argue. "But you've no idea how many women I've gone to bed with over the past nine years trying to forget you, Nora."

"I don't want to hear about all your other women."

"That's fine with me, since I don't want to talk about them." He ran his palm down her hair. "Your hair has always reminded me of corn silk." Memories of it draped across his naked chest, after making love, made his already aroused body hard.

"I suppose you tell that to all your women."

"I thought we'd agreed not to talk about other women."

"Although what you do and who you do it with isn't any of my business, as a doctor I have to point out that casual sex is dangerous, Caine. Especially these days."

"True enough. But you know, Nora, sex was never casual with you." His fingers curled around the back of her neck, his warm dark blue eyes captured her wary ones.

"Don't you think I know how uncomfortable this is for you?" he said in a low rough voice. "But it's not exactly a picnic for me, either, babe. Because right now my life is really messed up, and I have this feeling that if you and I could at least try to put the past to rest, maybe I'll be able to handle whatever the future brings."

"Besides—" he took hold of her hand, brought it to his lips and kissed her fingertips, one at a time "—we're still emotionally linked, Nora, whether we want to be or not."

"That's ridiculous."

"Why don't you kiss me again and try telling me that?"

She might be reckless whenever Caine was around, but Nora wasn't a complete idiot. "You've always been a good kisser, Caine. But then, practice makes perfect."

"It helps," he said easily. "Want to practice some more?"

"I just want to go home. I've had a long day."

"Come out to the cabin and I'll massage your feet. You used to like that."

Too much, Nora agreed silently. During their ill-fated marriage she'd reluctantly come to like far too many things about this man.

"You may be right about putting the past behind us," she agreed. "You're also probably right about us leaving a lot of things unsaid and saying a lot of things we didn't mean. But so help me God, if you so much as touch my feet, or any other part of my anatomy, Caine O'Halloran, I'll walk away and never speak to you again."

"You drive a hard bargain, Doc."

She lifted her chin. "Take it or leave it."

Caine rubbed his jaw thoughtfully, considering her ultimatum. Nora would come to him, he vowed. And not because of any past sexual memory and not because of any shared grief. She would come because of the same aching need he'd been suffering since that suspended, sensual moment in her examining room.

"You're on," he said. "I promise, on my word as a former Eagle Scout and New York Yankee, not to pounce on Dr. Nora Anderson O'Halloran."

His words were carefully chosen to remind her that they'd once shared the same name. Along with the same apartment, and more important, the same warm double bed.

Caine watched the awareness rise in her eyes again; he was not all that surprised when it was just as quickly banked.

"I haven't been Nora O'Halloran for nine years, Caine." She glanced at his car. "You go ahead in the Batmobile. I'll follow you out to the cabin."

"You know," Caine said casually, as if the thought had just occurred to him, "Dana dropped by the cabin with some Dungeness crab. Why don't you stay for dinner? We'll have them with rice pilaf. And a tomato-mozzarella salad with honey vinaigrette, topped off by a nice, unpretentious little bottle of Fumé Blanc."

"Rice pilaf? And honey vinaigrette? Is this the same man who had trouble boiling a hot dog?"

"I bought a cookbook especially written for the kitchen-impaired this afternoon." He didn't add that he'd purchased it specifically in the hopes of persuading Nora to have an intimate dinner with him. "It's got full-color photographs and everything. How about helping me to try it out?"

Nora thought about the frozen dinner waiting to be nuked in the microwave. "All right. Fresh crab sounds delicious. And I can't pass up the opportunity to see you in an apron."

"I'll do my best not to disappoint." He dug into his

pocket, pulled out his keys and slid one brass key off the ring. "Here's the front door key. I'll just stop at the store for the wine, rice and tomatoes and be right behind you."

"Just remember," she warned as she took the key from his outstretched hand, "we're only going to talk. You promised not to pounce."

"Scout's honor." He lifted his fingers in the same pledge he'd given Johnny Baker earlier. "Although I refuse to be held responsible for any naughty ideas you might come up with once you get me alone."

Refusing to dignify that remark with a response, Nora climbed into her car and slammed the door.

Unrepentant, Caine began whistling "My Girl" as he sauntered over to his own black beast parked two spaces away.

8

CAINE'S CHALET-STYLE cabin was situated in a remote forest clearing, on the bank of a stream in a grove of silvertrunked aspen, nestled up against the slope of the Olympic Mountains. Behind the cabin was a small, unnamed glacial lake.

Much more than a typical rustic structure, the chalet had a soaring cathedral ceiling and an open balustrade leading to the upstairs loft. Adding to the sense of spaciousness was a panoramic wall of glass that thrust outward toward the forest like the prow of an ancient sailing ship.

From the outside, surrounded by a dazzling carpet of the same yellow, blue and white wildflowers Caine had brought to the cemetery, the cabin appeared warm and welcoming.

The inside, however, looked as if a hurricane had swept through it. Clothes were strewn over every available piece of furniture, and although he'd been home nearly two weeks, other clothing remained in open suitcases on the floor. The rest of the plank flooring was littered with newspapers—all opened to the sports pages.

Empty beer cans littered the tops of the tables along with glasses that had etched white rings into the pine. Nora was surprised and disappointed to see an oversize plastic ashtray overflowing with cigarette butts. Cobwebs hung in the ceiling corners; dust covered everything.

She went into the kitchen, where she found more empty beer cans and a distressing number of bourbon bottles. The only time she'd ever seen Caine drink hard liquor was after the accident that had taken their son's life. His drinking, which had begun the night Dylan died, had escalated daily, culminating in that horrid, drunken scene at the cemetery.

A pizza box was open on the counter, the two remaining pieces of pepperoni pizza cold and forgotten. In the refrigerator were three additional six-packs of beer, the crab her brother had given Caine, a taco wrapped in bright yellow waxed paper, a handful of individual plastic hot-sauce containers and a bowl of guacamole that looked like an organic-chemistry lab experiment gone awry.

This was a mistake, Nora thought. The one thing she'd always admired about Caine O'Halloran was his absolute, unwavering self-confidence. To think of him, hiding away out here, drinking too much, destroying his lungs, and clogging his arteries with fat and cholesterol as he ate his solitary meals from TV trays, was surprisingly painful.

She had just decided to leave when the unmistakable whine of the Ferrari's engine cut through the mountain silence. A moment later, she heard the car door slam and Caine burst into the cabin, his arms filled with brown paper bags.

"Sorry it took longer than I'd planned," he greeted with a cheerfulness that was at distinct odds with the bleakness of their surroundings. "But I figured I might as well pick up a few basics while I was at it."

"That's a good idea. Since you don't have enough food around here to feed a starving gerbil."

"Old Mother Hubbard's cupboard has gotten a bit bare."

"Unfortunately, you can't say the same thing about the bar," she countered. "It seems to be more than adequately stocked. And when did you start smoking?"

"A few weeks ago. And for the record, I don't know why the hell people do it. The stuff tastes like shit."

"Not to mention the little fact that cigarettes cause heart disease, lung cancer, emphysema—"

"And may result in fetal injury, premature birth and low birth weight," he cut in. He tried to make room on the cluttered counter for the grocery bags, then, giving up, put them on the floor instead. "I read all the labels, Doc."

"But you smoked them anyway."

"I'm probably the only guy my age who never tried smoking when he was a kid. I thought I might enjoy it. I didn't. So I quit. Okay?"

"Too bad you didn't quit the booze while you were at it," she retorted. "I should take you into the hospital morgue and show you what an alcoholic's liver looks like."

A stony expression came over his face. "I'm not an alcoholic. And I damn well don't need a show-and-tell lecture from you, Dr. Anderson."

"You need something. Because in case you haven't noticed, Caine, this place looks like a pigsty." She wrinkled her nose. "And it smells like a saloon!"

"I happen to like saloons." Caine knew he'd been spending far too much time in them lately, but he'd throw himself off the top of nearby Mount Olympus before admitting that to Nora.

They were standing toe-to-toe. "Well, *I* don't."

"If you don't like the way the place smells, why don't you open a damn window?"

"I'd rather leave!"

"Fine. Go ahead and leave. I'm used to eating alone."

"No wonder, the way you've been acting. And a woman had better be current on her vaccinations before she risks walking in the front door, because this place is a toxic-waste dump. I'm surprised the county health inspector hasn't condemned it."

Caine raked his hand through his hair. "Christ, I'd forgotten what a shrew you could be."

"Shrew?" Her voice rose. "You invited me all the way out here to call me a shrew?" Nora was trembling with a temper only this man had ever been able to ignite. "You're insufferable."

"And you're still absolutely gorgeous when you're furious."

She would not let him get away with this again. "You really need to work on your pickup lines, O'Halloran. Because that one went out with 'What's your sign?'"

"I do okay," he growled. "Besides, if I *were* in the market to pick up a woman, I sure as hell wouldn't waste my time with some flat-chested, acid-tongued nag."

A lesser woman would have been intimidated by his glare, but Nora threw up her chin and met his blistering look with a furious one of her own.

"Then we're even. Because the last thing I want in my life is some out-of-control, self-pitying over-the-hill jock with a Peter Pan complex!"

Her words reverberated around the kitchen like an unwelcome echo. Caine was looming over her, forcing her to tilt her head back to see his eyes. He was angry—more than angry. He was as furious as Nora had ever seen him.

Caine felt a fresh surge of fury and welcomed it. He'd been going through the motions since realizing he was going to be put on waivers. How long had it been since he'd allowed himself to experience pure, unadulterated emotion? Too long.

A muscle jerked in his jaw. They glared at one another, each daring the other to make the next move.

"You know, your aim has gotten a helluva lot more accurate," Caine said finally. "Because you definitely scored a direct hit with that one, Nora."

They'd had too many of these fights in the past. And although they'd eventually made up in bed, each argument, every cruel word, had succeeded in straining the already tenuous bonds of their marriage. Until finally, those ties had snapped.

"I didn't want to score any hit," she murmured, looking down at the floor. "I thought that's what this dinner was all about. To put the past behind us, not relive it, word by hurtful word."

His hands were far from steady as he brushed Nora's bangs off her forehead. Caine wanted to try to make her understand the desperation that had led to his recent, admittedly less-than-ideal life-style. But how could he make her understand? When he still didn't understand himself?

"Hell. I'm sorry. Things have been a little rough lately. What with Maggie. And this damn arm and getting put on waivers. But I had no right to take my problems out on you."

"You just need to give it a bit more time," she advised. "Try a little patience."

"You know patience has never been my long suit."

"Would it be the end of the world," she asked quietly, "if you had to quit playing ball?"

"That's a moot point. Since I'm not finished."

A nagging doubt had been nibbling at the edges of his mind. Thus far, Caine had successfully ignored it. "If Nolan Ryan can pitch a no-hitter at forty-five, I'm damned if I'm going to admit to being washed up at thirty-five."

"You'll be thirty-six, next month."

"Okay, thirty-six. So who's counting?"

Everyone. And they both knew it.

Caine had been a ballplayer for as long as he could remember, and the one thing he refused to admit to Nora was that he didn't know how to separate the man from the athlete, even if he wanted to. Which he damn well didn't.

"Look, Nora," he said, trying to explain once again the one thing he'd never been able to make her understand, "I've spent my entire adult life, standing on a mound in front of a stadium of thousands and a television audience in the millions, expecting them to take me seriously for throwing a little piece of white cowhide at a stick.

"I know that to you, with your education and lofty profession, that seems like a ridiculous way to earn a living.

"But I throw that ball nearly a hundred miles an hour and I make a helluva lot of money for embarrassing some of the league's best hitters. I'm Caine the Giant Killer, and I love it. I love the competition. And I love to win."

"But your injury—"

He cut her off with an impatient wave of his hand. "Injuries are part of the game. And dammit, I refuse to allow a bit of bad luck to sidetrack me from a lifelong quest."

"I remember you were always questing after glory," she murmured. At the same time, she'd been in her first year of medical school and struggling with morning sickness.

"It's more than glory. I feel I have something left to achieve."

"So you're going to hang in there and keep swinging at the curveballs."

That earned a smile. "And if you swing at enough of them," he agreed, "eventually you'll hit a few out of the park. I hadn't realized you'd been listening in those days."

Just as she hadn't realized he'd been listening to her go on and on about medical school. Nora wondered if perhaps she'd misjudged him back then. Perhaps, she considered now, they'd misjudged one another.

"But I didn't ask you here to talk about baseball—" Caine's low voice broke into her thoughts "—or my injury." He slid his hand beneath her hair to cup her neck and hold her to his darkening gaze, making her nerve endings sizzle.

"How about a temporary truce?" he asked quietly.

The brief hot argument had left her drained. Nora wanted to lean her head against his broad shoulder; she wanted to wrap her arms around his waist and feel his strong arms around her, reassuring her that they could put this fight behind them, as they had so many others.

In the end, she released a slow, ragged breath and nodded. "Truce," she whispered.

She reached up and traced the planes of his face with her fingertips. Frowning at the yellowish bruise around his eye, she said, "Your eye still looks horrendous."

"It'll heal. They always do."

She shook her head in mute frustration. "You really haven't changed." Her faint smile took the sting out of her words.

Her stroking touch was beginning to drive him crazy. Unable to keep from touching her, Caine ran his palms up and down her arms. "Ah, we're back to my Peter Pan complex."

"I shouldn't have said that."

He shrugged. "I shouldn't have called you a shrew." Lightly he traced her ear and played with her pearl earring.

"Don't forget the 'flat-chested, acid-tongued nag.'"

Caine had the good grace to flush at that one. "Definitely uncalled-for." His finger trailed down her throat. "Your chest is just right."

The finger crossed her collarbone. "In fact, I remember thinking, that first time here in the cabin, how perfectly your breasts fit my palms and wondering if everything between us would be such a close and perfect fit."

With deliberate leisure, the treacherous finger glided over her breast. "And it was." Just as she felt herself slipping under his seductive spell, the beeper in her coat pocket buzzed; its screen displayed the emergency-code number. Saved by the bell. Again.

She called the hospital from the kitchen phone, then turned back to Caine. He was leaning against the counter, his long legs crossed at the ankles, watching her with unwavering intensity.

"I have to go."

He wasn't surprised; her relief at the untimely interruption had been palpable. With uncommon self-control, Caine managed not to complain as he followed Nora out to her car.

"How about coming back after you're finished with your emergency?" Behind her, the rays of the sunset spread out over the Olympic Mountains like an enormous scarlet fan.

"I don't think that would be a very good idea."

"Why not?"

"Because I have no idea how long I'll be." Her hand remained firmly on the car door handle, as if to anchor herself against the storm of emotions swirling inside her.

"I don't mind waiting." Uncurling her fingers from the door handle, he took her hand in his.

"I wouldn't want you to have to do that. Especially

when it could take all night." She forced a smile. "But there will be other chances to talk before you leave town."

"You know I want to do more than talk, Nora."

"Yes." Her eyes were painfully grave. "And to tell you the truth, back in there—" she tossed her head in the direction of the cabin "—I was tempted. But I think what's happening here doesn't really have anything to do with us, Caine.

"I think deep inside you there's a voice saying that if you could only turn the clock back to when you were younger, to those days when you and I were married and you first got called up to the majors, perhaps you could start pitching the way you once did again, too."

He lifted a challenging brow. "Now you're a shrink?"

"No. But it doesn't take a psychology degree to see that you're dealing with a lot of difficult issues, Caine. As your doctor, and your friend, I'd suggest you try to take things more slowly."

With that, she pulled her hand free, climbed into the driver's seat, closed the door, fastened her seat belt and drove away from the cabin.

Caine stood at the end of the driveway, hands shoved into his pockets, and watched Nora leave. Timing, he considered grimly, as he trudged back up to the cabin, was everything.

He went back into the cabin, swore as he glanced at the bags of groceries, then picked up a bottle of bourbon and walked down to the dock.

The night grew cool. A gentle mist that wasn't quite rain began to fall. Caine sat alone, on the end of his dock, drinking his way through the Jack Daniel's.

He'd told himself that he'd come down here to think, but that was a lie. He'd come down here to get roaring drunk.

The problem was, Caine realized, holding the bottle up toward the crescent moon to determine the level of the remaining bourbon, it wasn't working.

Oh, he knew that if he suddenly stood his legs wouldn't be all that steady, that the dock would appear to be swaying. But while the alcohol was undoubtedly having its effect on his body, his mind was, unfortunately, distressingly clear.

He tipped the bottle to his lips. Flames slid down his throat and spread thickly, soothingly, in his stomach as he thought back to the afternoon when he'd finally made love to Nora for the second time.

They'd been married for six months that week, but neither had thought to celebrate the anniversary. After all, theirs had not been a conventional marriage. It had been a practical arrangement, a contract entered into by both parties for their mutual benefit. Nothing more.

At least that was what he'd been telling himself. Until that fateful day when his life had inexorably changed. He'd been eating a pizza and drinking beer while watching television when Nora burst into the apartment, her eyes red from crying. She ran past him into the bedroom as if he were invisible, slamming the door behind her. A moment later, Caine heard the sound of water running in the bathroom, the buzz of her electric toothbrush, then the unmistakable sound of weeping.

He lowered the beer can to the coffee table and sat there, debating what to do next. Part of him opted for ignoring the incident.

But another, stronger part of him couldn't overlook the fact that something was definitely wrong. When he thought that it might have something to do with the baby, his blood chilled.

He'd pointed the remote control at the screen; the

screen went black. Realizing that his breath undoubtedly reeked of beer and pepperoni, and remembering how she'd looked a little queasy this morning, Caine dug a lint-covered peppermint out of his jeans pocket and popped it into his mouth.

Then he crossed the living room and opened the bedroom door.

"Nora?" The room was dark but he could see her, curled up in a fetal position on the bed. "What's wrong?"

"Go away." She was hugging a pillow against her; her words were muffled by the foam.

"Not until I find out if anything's wrong with the baby."

"The baby's fine."

But she wasn't. And that disturbed the hell out of him. Caine crossed the room. The mattress sank under his weight as he sat down beside her. "You want to tell me what happened?"

"No."

He could feel her trembling. "Come on, Nora." Feeling awkward, he smoothed her hair with his palm. "Whatever it is, it can't be all that bad."

To his surprise, Nora Anderson O'Halloran, the same woman who'd taken extra pains to avoid so much as accidentally brushing against him in their cramped apartment, had suddenly sat up, flung her arms around his neck and pressed her wet face into his shirt.

"Oh, Caine!" She lifted her doe brown eyes that were dark and heartbreakingly bleak. "I'm never going to be a doctor!"

"Of course you are."

"Not after what I did in gross anatomy class today."

"What did you do? Make a slip with the scalpel and emasculate Irving?"

Irving was the cadaver her anatomy study group had been laboring over.

When he'd first heard about the class, Caine had thought the term "gross anatomy" a perfect description. Eventually, he'd become accustomed to the fact that his wife spent her mornings with a dead body the same way he'd grown used to the faint odor of formaldehyde lingering in her blond hair.

"It's n-n-not funny," she insisted on a tortured breath.

"I'm sorry." Caine tried to understand. "What happened?"

"My morning sickness came back today."

"I thought you looked a little under the weather at breakfast," Caine remembered. "But didn't Dr. Palmer tell you that might happen if you got too tired?"

"Yes. But, oh, y-y-you don't understand." Her shoulders slumped defeatedly.

"I'm trying." Caine lifted her chin on a finger and looked into her red-rimmed eyes. "But you're not exactly a font of information, Nora."

"It's s-s-so embarrassing." She dashed at the moisture stinging her eyes and shook her head in a violent gesture.

Comprehension dawned. "You threw up in class."

Nora gave him a weary look. "All over Irving's inferior v-v-vena c-cava."

Caine had absolutely no idea what an inferior vena cava was and decided that it probably didn't really matter. Not to Irving anymore, anyway.

"Is that all?" Caine gave Nora an encouraging smile. "I seem to recall you telling me about three students who tossed their cookies the first week of class."

"That was the first week," Nora explained soberly. "By now we're all supposed to be used to it."

Personally, Caine thought he could probably spend the

rest of his life with Irving and not get used to the idea of cutting into human organs—dead or alive—but he knew that was not the point of this conversation.

If he were to be perfectly fair, he'd have to acknowledge that Nora probably couldn't imagine the pure pleasure of watching a batter hit a pop fly off your curveball, either. "You're pregnant. I'm sure your professor will take that into consideration."

"Dr. Eugene Fairfield is an antiquated old fossil who doesn't believe women belong in medicine, period," she muttered. "As for pregnant women...." She sighed. "And it gets worse. After I got sick, I fainted."

"Fainted?" Fear raced through him as his hand dropped to her belly, rounded with his child. "Are you sure you're okay?"

"Yes. I was only out for a second, and the only person who got hurt was Irving."

"How the hell could Irving get hurt?"

"I pulled the table over when I fell and the next thing I knew, Irving was sprawled on the floor, with his gall bladder and his liver lying beside him."

Nora drew in a deep, shuddering breath. "I know Dr. Fairfield's going to flunk me and I'll get kicked out of medical school and I'll never be a doctor!"

Moisture flooded her eyes again and she clung to him, sobbing harshly into his shoulder.

If he hadn't been so genuinely distressed, Caine would have laughed at the idea of quiet, studious Nora, of all people, causing such havoc in class.

But she was more distraught than he'd ever seen her. And, staggered by her misery, Caine rocked her in his arms and murmured inarticulate words of comfort into her ear.

His hands moved up and down her back, the gesture

meant to comfort, rather than arouse. His lips pressed against her hair and caught the soft scent of flowers beneath the aroma of formaldeyhde she'd brought with her from the lab.

After an immeasurable time, Caine could tell by Nora's slow steady breathing that her pain had run its course.

"Feeling better?"

"Yes." Her soft eyes mirrored her surprise as she tilted her head back and looked up at him. "I am. Thank you."

Her quiet formality along with the lingering pain in her eyes had tugged at something elemental deep inside him. Looking down into her pale and unusually open face, Caine was engulfed with a tenderness like nothing he'd ever known.

And with that tenderness, he realized, came love.

"You don't have to thank me, Nora." His gaze moved over her pale, uplifted face. "I'm your husband. And although I'll admit to being a little vague about husbandly duties, I think a shoulder to cry on comes with the job."

"But we agreed—"

"I don't give a damn what we agreed." She'd pointed out the terms of their agreement innumerable times over the past six months and Caine was sick of hearing it. "Would it be against the rules if I kissed you?"

Surprise warred with unwilling desire on her lovely features. "I think it would."

"Too bad." Bending his head, he kissed her face where salty tears were still drying.

"Caine—"

"What, Nora?" His lips skimmed along the slanted line of her cheekbone.

"I don't think this is a very good idea."

"You might be right." His teeth closed around the tender skin of her earlobe and Nora drew in a quick breath but did not pull away. "But I can't come up with a logical reason why I shouldn't make love to my wife."

With a sensitivity neither had been aware of him possessing, his hand moved slowly, possessively, from her shoulder to her belly. "How about you?"

"No." Nora's soft breathless voice was a whisper of surrender. "I can't." With a sigh, she closed her eyes, relaxed and let him guide her into the mists.

His hands slipped under her maternity top, unhooked the front clasp of her bra with ease and cupped her breasts. When his thumb brushed against her nipple, Nora gasped and would have pulled away. But before she could move, Caine's lips fused to hers.

Caine felt the last vestiges of her resistance ebb. He felt it in the softening of her lips and the strength of her fingers as she clutched his upper arms. Heat simmered at the base of his spine, making him ache.

He pulled off her oversize blouse and tossed it onto the floor. Her nipples, which he remembered as being a rosy pink, had darkened to the hue of the cranberries that grew wild in bogs along the coast. And they were just as hard, Caine discovered as he brushed his hand over one dusky bud. The intimate touch made Nora stiffen in his arms. "Don't worry," he soothed. "I promise not to take you anywhere you don't want to go, Nora."

Passively, she relaxed again. Sensing her trust, Caine took pains not to abuse it. Slowly, banking the rising desire born of six long and lonely months of celibacy, he ran whisper-soft kisses across her lips, from one corner of her mouth to the other, before going on to kiss her cheeks, her forehead, her temple, the bridge of her nose.

All the time, his fingers circled her breasts, caressing, stroking. Caine could feel her pulse beginning to thunder;

still he took his time, determined not to succumb to any quick burst of pleasure.

"I've been going crazy, thinking about this." His tongue traced a line from her throat down to her breasts. "Remembering the sweet, sexy taste of your skin." When he took a nipple between his teeth and tugged, she gasped, then arched against him. "How you turn to liquid silk in my arms."

"Oh, Caine." The softly spoken name seemed to echo off the wall, surrounding them. Embracing them. "Tell me," she whispered. "Tell me everything you've been thinking."

"Everything?" He wove his fingers into her hair, holding her gaze with his. "Are you sure a woman in your delicate condition is up to some of my more graphic fantasies?"

"Why don't you try me and see?" she suggested with a smile that managed to be both shy and seductive at the same time.

"All right." He coaxed her onto her back and skimmed a trail of wet, openmouthed kisses down her rib cage. "But don't say I didn't warn you."

Her maternity jeans had a jersey insert to allow room for her expanding belly. The jeans were, Caine considered, highly practical and decidedly unsexy. After unbuttoning them at the waist, he began pulling them slowly down her legs.

What he found beneath the durable denim came as a distinct surprise. "Black silk?"

"They were a wedding present from Karin." Nora's cheeks flamed.

"I think I like these a lot better than the pots and pans my parents gave us." Caine smoothed his hands over her stomach, where the child—their child, he thought wonderingly—had been growing all these months. Imbued with tenderness, he pressed his lips against her flesh.

Then, moving on, Caine slipped his fingers beneath the lace-trimmed legs and inched upward to secret pleasures. "Remind me to thank your sister-in-law, first chance I get."

"Don't you dare!"

"It won't do any good to pretend to be scandalized, my dear wife." He lowered his mouth and drew a wet swath just above the waistband of the low-rise panties with his tongue. "Because any woman who'd wear panties like this in your condition is a wild woman at heart."

"I must be." Nora combed her hands through Caine's hair and writhed beneath his increasingly intimate touch. "Because this is just about all I've been thinking about lately."

"Really?" The admission brought a burst of male pride.

"Really. My obstetrician says it's raging hormones, but I'm not so sure she's right."

He dipped his tongue into her navel. "Then what do you think has been making you all hot and bothered lately?"

"I don't know."

She was lying. Caine could read it in her eyes. Apparently he wasn't the only one who'd found forced celibacy a burden.

"Perhaps you've been reading my mind." He lay down beside her and cupped her breast. "Perhaps you tuned in on how much I wanted to taste you again." He took the hardened nipple into his mouth, causing a moan of pleasure to slip past her lips.

The soft moan brought a fresh surge of arousal—one Caine managed, with effort, to bank.

"Maybe you knew how I've been imagining the feel of

your body against mine." He yanked his T-shirt over his head and pulled her against him, heated flesh against heated flesh. "And how the thought of you, hot and wet, makes me hard."

He took her hand and pressed it against the placket of his jeans, letting her feel the full extent of his need. "See how much I want you?"

"I've tried to understand," she murmured with reluctant wonder. Her fingers began stroking his burgeoning flesh through the thick material. "I've lain awake nights trying to analyze why everything's so different with you, but I can't come up with a logical answer."

"Then don't think." With fingers that were not as steady as he would have liked, Caine unfastened the five-button jeans, vowing to go out and buy a pair with a zipper as soon as the stores opened in the morning. "Don't analyze. Just feel."

The room was washed in shadows. A full moon rose in the sky outside the bedroom, bathing the lovers in a soft silvery light. But still Caine refused to rush.

Even when they were laying together, naked, he kept his own flaming hunger tightly reined as his hands continued to stroke and his lips took long, leisurely tours over her body—her rounded stomach, the small of her back, her shoulders, that sensitive spot he'd discovered on her ankle—always to return again and again to her soft, pliant lips.

When he finally slipped into her, a deep current of love flowed through him, like a river, and he realized how fulfilling tenderness could be.

Very soon after that day, Nora's obstetrician had cautioned against engaging in intercourse. But that hadn't stopped them from exploring myriad other imaginative ways to pleasure one another. Nora was the only woman

Caine had ever met who could actually be brought to orgasm by nibbling on the tendon at the back of her knee.

And he was positive that she was one of the few women who'd ever climaxed during labor. At the time, he'd only been trying to take her mind off her pain. But when his stroking hand had moved under the hospital sheet, beyond her undulating belly and between her legs, to recklessly toy with the hard pink nubbin of flesh, Nora had cried out, not in pain, but in absolute, stunned pleasure. Her noisy response had brought the nurse, who, after examining her, had found her not fully dilated. The nurse had patted Nora's head in a maternal way, and told her to go ahead and yell whenever she felt the urge.

The moment she'd left the room in a rustle of starched cotton, Nora and Caine had collapsed in gales of shared laughter.

The memories made Caine's body throb. He tipped the bottle back, only to discover it was empty. "Damn."

Cursing inarticulately, he flung it into the lake, struggled to his feet and wove his way back to the cabin.

He staggered across the living room and crashed onto the newspaper-strewn sofa. The painkillers were on the coffee table where he'd left them that first night. Caine picked up the plastic bottle, shook a handful of the pink pills into his palm and stared blearily down at them.

What would happen if he just said the hell with everything and swallowed them all? It would, he considered for a fleeting second, solve a hell of a lot of problems.

Except he couldn't do it. He might be nothing but a drunk, washed-up ballplayer with two failed marriages behind him, but he damn well didn't want his fans to remember him as a coward.

Cursing, he flung the tablets away. They scattered over

the clothes-covered floor and were immediately forgotten.

Then, exhausted by the too-vivid memories and numbed by too much alcohol, Caine fell instantly into a deep sleep.

9

"WHAT IN THE BLAZES do you think you're doing, Caine O'Halloran?"

Maggie crossed her arms over her chest, where a trio of pilot whales swam against the bright blue background of today's sweatshirt. "Chasing after Nora Anderson when you've already got yourself a wife back in New York City."

"Now, Maggie," Devlin soothed as he put a cup of coffee down in front her. "Don't you think you're bein' a little hard on the boy?"

"That's just my point," Maggie snapped. "Caine is not a boy. He's a grown man with a wife."

"Tiffany and I are getting a divorce."

Caine took a bite of one of the glazed doughnuts Devlin had brought to the table along with the coffee. He'd come to turn over his grandmother's garden, a spring ritual Maggie was definitely not up to this year.

Maggie frowned at Caine over the rim of her mug. "Even if that's the case, like it or not, the law still says you're a married man, Caine. Which means you have no business chasing after Nora."

"I wasn't chasing after her," Caine argued. "Hell, after Harmon beat me up, Dana and Tom took me to the clinic to have her patch me up."

"You're not going to try to tell me that you invited her to your cabin the other night for medical reasons, are you?

I may be old, but I'm not senile. Least, not yet," Maggie muttered.

Caine silently cursed Trudy down at the market. The woman had the biggest mouth in town. Second biggest, he amended, remembering Ingrid Johansson.

"I invited her to the cabin for dinner. And to talk."

"It's still not right, Caine," Maggie said. "It isn't fair to your wife. And it damn well isn't fair to Nora."

"But—"

"Better hear your grandmother out, Caine," Devlin said in a quiet but firm tone.

"All right." Feeling like he had when he was nine years old and had accidentally driven Maggie's Cessna twin engine through the side of the hangar, Caine tilted the kitchen chair back on its rear legs, crossed his outstretched legs at the ankle and waited. "Fire away."

Maggie nodded, satisfied that she had his undivided attention. "Now, I'm not saying there's anything wrong with your feelings for Nora. Everyone in town can see that you and that girl are ripe for a second chance. And the way things ended the last time, Lord knows you both deserve one.

"But you were brought up to do the right thing, Caine. And courtin' your first wife while you're still married to your second one just isn't the right thing to do."

"Even if it feels right?" he couldn't help asking.

Maggie's stern gaze softened for a moment. "If everybody did what felt right at the time, Caine, the world would be in an even worse pickle than it is now."

"You gotta choose, Caine," Devlin advised. "One wife or the other."

"Hell, there's no choice." Caine dropped the chair back on all four legs. "I want Nora." The moment he heard himself say the words out loud, Caine knew they were true.

"Then take care of your problem with the other one," Maggie instructed. "This Tiffany. And then, when you're free, you can do whatever it takes to get Nora back."

"Speaking about doing the right thing," Caine ventured carefully, "I've been talking to Nora about you."

Maggie's expressive face instantly closed. "You had no right doin' that, Caine."

"I've every right. I love you and I can't stand by and watch you..."

"Die?" Maggie finished matter-of-factly, when Caine couldn't say it.

"Don't you see," Caine said, leaning forward, his own problems momentarily forgotten, "you don't have to give up, Gram. I've got more money than I can count—"

"I told her about the three million," Devlin broke in.

"And it's a right nice piece of change," Maggie allowed. "Your pappy and I are real proud of you, Caine."

"Thank you. But the point is that all the money doesn't mean a damn thing if I can't make life better for my family."

"Our lives are pretty good the way they are, boy," Devlin said quietly.

"But if you had a new heart, Gram..."

"I like the heart I've got just fine," she told him briskly. "It's served me right well for eighty-two years."

Maggie pushed herself up from the table and came over to stand beside him. Her always-wiry frame looked heartbreakingly frail. But the feisty determination gleaming in her blue eyes reminded Caine of a bantam rooster.

He rose and gathered the small woman into his arms. "Nora told me she'd talked to you about a hospice program. Will you at least take her advice about that?"

Maggie tilted her head back to meet his entreating gaze. "I'll think about it."

Well, it wasn't the answer he'd wanted, but, Caine told himself, it was a start.

"On one condition," Maggie warned.

"I figured there'd be a catch."

"There usually is with your grandmother," Devlin murmured knowingly.

"I want you to stop actin' like a crazy damn fool," Maggie insisted. "It's time you stopped drinking and drivin' too fast and gettin' into fistfights and whorin' around."

She poked a bony finger into his chest—a vivid reminder that she hadn't always been so weak. "Nora Anderson is a nice, sensible girl. She deserves a whole lot better than the idiot you've been since you came back to town. So it's high time you straightened up and flew right."

She wasn't telling him anything he hadn't been telling himself. Truthfully, Caine had been finding his recent lifestyle depressing.

There'd been a time, in his admittedly reckless youth, when he could party like a wild man all night, then show up at the ballpark and blaze that little white ball a hundred miles an hour past a stunned batter. But no more.

Maybe, he considered, he really was getting old. Lord, that was a depressing thought.

Refusing to consider such a negative idea when he already had enough problems to work out, Caine reached down and ruffled Maggie's pink-and-silver hair affectionately.

"Okay, Gram," he said, flashing her the bold smile that had brightened the cover of *Sports Illustrated* on three separate occasions. "You've got yourself a deal."

LATER THAT AFTERNOON, seeking companionship, Caine drove to the hospital to visit Johnny Baker. He dumped his purchases—an enormous bag of buttered popcorn, a six-pack of cola and a red-and-white-striped peanut bag—on the rollaway table. Then, making himself comfortable, he sprawled out on the vacant bed.

They were watching television when Nora entered the room.

"Hi, Dr. Anderson," Johnny greeted her. "The Yankees are playing the Twins," he explained, his enthusiasm a vast contrast to the dispirited little boy who'd shown up at her emergency room. "And boy, are they gettin' stomped. They need Caine real bad."

"I'm sure they do," she murmured absently. "How are you feeling, Johnny?" She crossed the room, picked up the remote control from the rumpled sheet, pointed it at the screen and muted the audio.

"I've been kinda lonely. This is a big place and the nurses are too busy with all the sick little kids to come visit me. But I'm feelin' a lot better," Johnny assured her. "Now that Caine's here."

"I'm surprised you don't have a major stomachache," Nora said, looking pointedly at the peanut shells scattered over the table and the bed.

"Can't watch a baseball game without the proper food, Doc," Caine said easily. "It's downright un-American."

"The hospital dietician would have a heart attack if she walked into this room right now."

"Caine just wanted to cheer me up," Johnny argued. The color drained from his face as if he feared she might send his hero away. "Please don't get mad at him, Dr. Anderson."

"I'm not angry at Caine." She flashed the seven-year-old an encouraging smile. "I hear we're losing you this afternoon."

"Yeah." He didn't sound very eager. "The social-worker lady found me a foster home."

"I know. She told me they were nice people."

"Yeah, that's what she told me, too." He sighed.

"Worried?"

"Kinda." He looked up at her, a tense white line around his mouth. "What if they don't like me?"

"Of course they'll like you. You're a terrific kid, Johnny," Caine assured him.

"Caine's right. All the nurses say you're one of the best they've ever had on the ward," Nora added.

"Really?"

"Really. And I agree," she said. "One hundred percent."

There was a little silence as Johnny thought about that.

"Besides," Nora continued, "you don't think an important ballplayer like Caine O'Halloran would spend so much time with a kid who wasn't terrific, do you?"

Johnny chewed his bottom lip as he considered that. Apparently satisfied, he announced, "Caine's going to Canada."

Nora shot Caine a surprised glance. "Oh?"

"I was going to stop by your office and change my appointment to get the stitches out." Caine wondered if it was disappointment he saw in her guarded gaze and hoped like hell it was. "I'm flying some guys up for a few days of fishing so Gram won't lose her charter fee."

"His grandmother's sick," Johnny offered.

"I know." Nora knew Maggie had started Caine flying young. He'd earned his private pilot's license before he was old enough for a driver's permit. "That's a nice thing to do."

He shrugged. "It's not as if I'm real busy these days. Besides, it's an excuse to go fishing and get paid for it."

"When Caine gets back, he's takin' me flying."

A light gleamed in Johnny's eyes and Nora knew that Caine was responsible for putting it there. She'd seen that same pleasure in Dylan's eyes, in what seemed like a lifetime ago.

That her son had adored his father had always been obvious. And it had been just as obvious that Caine had loved his little boy.

"Caine, may I speak with you? Outside?"

"Sure." He slid off the bed, rumpling the sheets even more. "I'll be back in a flash, sport." He tugged on the brim of the autographed Yankees cap, then turned it around backward.

It was only a casual gesture, but it made Johnny's eyes turn as adoring as a cocker spaniel's. "Don't be too long. The seventh-inning stretch'll be over in a minute."

Nora returned the remote to Johnny, who immediately turned on the sound.

"I'm really sorry about the popcorn, Nora," Caine said when they were alone in the waiting room at the end of the hallway. "It seemed like a good idea at the time."

"This isn't a playground, Caine. It's a hospital. And Johnny's my patient."

"But you're the one who said that there wasn't really anything physically wrong with the kid. I figured a little TLC never hurt anyone."

"TLC? Is that what you call it?"

"Okay, how about attention? Is that a better word?"

"That child has been through hell. I will not let you hurt him."

"Hurt him?" Caine's brows climbed his tanned forehead. "I was trying to help, Nora."

"Right now Johnny's proving a pleasant enough little diversion for you. But what about if you get called back to the majors—"

"When."

"What?" She dragged a frustrated hand through her hair.

"You said, *if* I get called back. I was merely clarifying that the proper phrasing was *when* I return to major-league ball."

"When, if—the words don't matter," she said, brushing his correction away with a furious wave of her hand. "The point is that Johnny's going to start to care for you, and count on you, and maybe even love you, and you're going to abandon him, just like—"

She cut her words off in midsentence, but the damage had already been done. Caine would have had to be dense as a stump not to get her drift.

"Like I abandoned you?" he asked quietly.

"That's not what I was going to say." It was a lie and they both knew it.

"Look, I'll be the first to admit that marriage wasn't high on my list of priorities ten years ago, Nora.

"But that day you embarrassed yourself in anatomy class by tossing your cookies all over Irving, I realized that somehow, when I wasn't looking, you'd become much, much more."

"What happened between us is in the past, Caine."

"Now why can't I believe that?"

"Believe it." She turned to leave, then stopped long enough to give him a warning. "And don't you dare hurt Johnny Baker."

With that, she marched away.

Caine wanted to go after her. But remembering his pledge to Maggie, he sighed and returned to watch the rest of the game with the one person in Tribulation who wasn't asking more than he could deliver.

Five days later, Caine was back in Tribulation, sitting in a window booth in the Timberline Café, watching the rain streak down the glass, when Nora walked in.

"Hi." She stopped beside the table.

"Hi, yourself."

"So how was the fishing?"

"Terrific. Of course, Fortress Lake is easy; you could catch a boatful of Eastern brook trout on peanut-butter-and-jelly sandwiches."

"You probably stocked your freezer, then."

"Naw. Except for the fish we cooked each night for dinner, and one mounted trophy per paying guest, we put the rest back."

"Oh. That's nice."

The polite conversation trailed off, but neither one moved. Caine sat looking up at her while Nora looked down at him; both were oblivious to the interested quiet that had settled over the café.

"I heard from Social Services that Johnny's settling into his foster home," she said.

"I know. I stopped by to see him on the way home from the airport."

"How's he getting along?"

"Great. When I left, he was rolling on the lawn with a litter of six-week-old golden retriever puppies." His lips curved into a reminiscent smile. "You should have seen him, Nora. He looked just like any other kid."

"You've had a lot to do with that," she said. "I'm not sure he ever would have opened up to that social worker if you hadn't encouraged him."

Caine shrugged. "It wasn't that big a deal."

"It was to Johnny." She combed her fingers through her

hair in a nervous gesture he remembered too well. "I owe you an apology. For what I said the other day. About you hurting him."

"You were only thinking of Johnny," Caine said without rancor. "Did you know his mother is putting him up for adoption?"

"I heard this morning."

Caine shook his head. "Helluva thing, giving up your own child. But I suppose it's for the best. For Johnny."

"I think it probably is," Nora agreed.

There was another poignant silence as they studied each other.

Nora searched for something, anything, to say. "I see you're working on your second five gallons," she said finally, looking down at his mug.

The white mug, which bore Caine's name in black block print, proclaimed that he was a member of Ingrid's five-gallon club.

It took one hundred cups of coffee to make five gallons, and once a customer made the quota, he got his own mug. The mugs stayed on a shelf on the back wall; the fact that Caine's had been waiting for him all these years was additional proof that some things never changed.

"Every man needs a goal," Caine answered easily. "Pappy comes here every morning. Says that if his mug's on the shelf, he knows he's still alive."

Nora laughed even as she felt a bittersweet pain. "I was by their house yesterday. Maggie was looking well."

Caine's jaw tensed. "For someone who's now bedridden."

"Oh, Caine." Feeling his frustration, she put a comforting hand on his shoulder. Refusing to consider whether or not it was a wise or safe thing to do, he raised his own to cover hers.

They exchanged another long, heartfelt look. Somewhere in the background, Nora heard the sound of bells.

"Caine..."

"Nora..."

They spoke at the same time, then laughed uneasily.

"Ladies first," Caine said.

Before Nora could respond, Ingrid, who'd been watching the exchange along with the others, called out to her. "Nora, telephone."

Forgetting that they had an audience, forgetting that such unruly feelings were inordinately risky, Nora struggled against breaking the spell. "Could you please take a message, Ingrid," she asked softly, not taking her eyes from Caine's face.

"I think you'd better take this one, Nora," Ingrid insisted.

Hearing the strain in the elderly woman's voice, Nora dragged her gaze from Caine's. Concern was etched into every deep line of Ingrid Johansson's face.

When she took the receiver from Ingrid, a foreboding chill ran up Nora's spine. "Hello?"

"Thank God I found you." Her brother's voice, ragged and hurried, came over the wire.

"What's wrong?"

"Tom called. Eric is missing," Dana said.

"Missing?" She sagged against Caine, who, having seen the color leave her face, had come up behind her. "How? Where?"

"According to Tom, he was on a scout hike at Lake Crescent. He got separated from the group and then a squall came up. All the other kids got back to the cabins safe and sound. The sheriff and the Park Service are organizing a search party."

"Are they at the lodge?"

"Yeah. The troop rented a couple of the cabins, but the command post is being set up in the lodge lobby. I'll meet you there."

"I'm leaving now." She thrust the phone toward Ingrid and turned, prepared to run toward the door.

Caine took hold of Nora's elbow and felt her tremors. "Let's go."

Set dramatically among the lushly forested northern ridges of the Olympic Mountains, Lake Crescent had long been considered the gem of the peninsula's many scenic attractions.

Although Native American legend taught that Lake Crescent was created when Mountain Storm King, angered by a fight that had broke out in Peaceful Valley, hurled part of his crest and dammed the river, geologists insisted on the more mundane explanation that a slow-moving glacier, gnawing at bedrock, had created the incredible blue-green lake.

The lake had been drawing tourists since the early 1890s; the two-story, shingled lodge had been constructed in 1915. Caine had enjoyed many weekend outings at the lake; today, however, the mood was anything but festive.

When he and Nora entered the lodge, Karin, who'd been standing by the stone fireplace, surrounded by a protective circle of friends, ran toward them.

"Thank God you're here!"

"You know there's nowhere else I'd be." Nora hugged her. "Everything's going to be all right. Eric's going to be found."

"I wish I could believe that." Karin turned to Caine.

"Hello, Caine," she said with a formal politeness that was so ill-suited to the occasion, Caine suspected that it was the only way she could keep from breaking into torrents of weeping. "Thank you for coming."

Caine gathered her into his arms, bent his head and brushed his lips against her temple. "How could I not?"

Tilting her head back, Karin bit her lip as new tears threatened. "Please find my little boy, Caine."

"We will," he promised roughly. "I promise." He handed her gently back to Nora, squeezed his former wife's shoulder comfortingly, then strode across the room to join the search team.

WHAT HAD BEEN A DREARY drizzle in Tribulation was a full-fledged squall at the lake. The cold wind howled off the steep slopes of the mountains; icy rain intermittently turned to sleet. The sky over the lake was as thick and dark as a wet wool blanket.

The searchers, working in teams of four, had been assigned sections: each section led in a different direction from the trail from which Eric had disappeared. As darkness descended on the mountains, the temperature dropped.

An icy rain dripped off the hood of his poncho as Caine searched; the yellow beam of his flashlight disappeared into the fog and mist.

The look of absolute fear in Karin's eyes had sliced at him like a sharp knife. It had been the same look he'd seen in Nora's eyes when she'd arrived at the emergency room that fateful day. The day Dylan...

No! Caine shook his head, spattering rain the way Ranger, his old springer spaniel, used to do when he'd gotten wet waiting with his master in a duck blind.

Never again would he listen to the sound of a human heart shattering. He was going to find Eric, dammit! He was.

It was then he heard a faint sound that could have been the wind whistling.

Caine stopped and gestured for the rest of his team to do the same. The sound grew more distinct. It was, Caine realized with a burst of relief, the unmistakable sobbing of a child.

They found Eric lying on a bed of needles beneath the spreading dark green arms of a towering Douglas fir. He was filthy and scared and exhausted. But, Caine determined as he ran his hands over the young body, unharmed.

"Uncle Caine? Is that really you?"

"It's me, all right." Caine scooped the eight-year-old into his arms. "Come on, sport," he said. "We're taking you home."

Two wet, dirty arms crept around Caine's neck. "I saw a fawn. I was following it when I got lost."

"That'll teach you to stick to the trail," Caine advised with a calm that belied the runaway pounding of his heart.

"I'm probably going to be in trouble, huh?"

"Your mom's real worried."

"Was she crying?"

"A little. When she sees you safe and sound, she'll probably cry a lot more."

"And then she'll ground me."

"I'd say that's a distinct possibility," Caine agreed. "But my grandpappy taught me, when I was about your age, that it's best just to take your medicine and get it over with."

"Yeah. That's what Dad always says," Eric said glumly.

"Of course, my gram taught me something else about medicine," Caine said.

"What?"

"That it always goes down smoother if you follow it with a spoonful of honey. So how about, after you get ungrounded, you and I go to Seattle and take in a Mariners game?"

"Really?"

"Really."

They entered the lodge with a gust of rain and wind. Caine, carrying Eric, was flanked by Dana and Joe Bob Carroll. Bring up the rear was Harmon Olson. Which wasn't all that unbelievable, Nora decided. Tribulation's citizens were the type of people who always pulled together in times of trouble. And a missing child was enough to make even the most long-term adversaries put aside their personal differences.

"Oh, Eric!"

Tears of joy coursing down her face, Karin ran toward Caine and flung her arms around both of them. "I was so worried." Her hands trembled as they moved over her son's dirt-caked face. "Are you all right?"

"I think he's fine," Caine answered. "Nora can confirm that, for sure."

"So worried," Karin repeated shakily. "I'm so happy to see you." She combed her hands through his tousled hair, dislodging fir needles. "You're grounded for a week."

Heaving a deep sigh, Eric exchanged an I-told-you-so look with his uncle over the top of his mother's pale blond head.

Feeling better than he had in ages, Caine threw back his head and laughed.

10

CAINE AND NORA DROVE back to Tribulation in weary, but comfortable silence.

"My car's at the Timberline," she remembered when he turned down the street toward her house.

"I'll bring it by tomorrow," he suggested. "You look beat. I thought you'd rather go straight home."

"I am tired." Nora glanced over his strong profile silhouetted in the slanting silver moonlight. "But I wasn't trudging around in the rain all night. You must be exhausted."

Caine pulled up in front of her grandmother's house and cut the engine. "Actually, I'm still a little wired."

They went up the front walk in silence, side by side, shoulders almost touching. The boards creaked underfoot as they climbed the five wooden steps to the porch. They stood there, facing one another in front of her door. "Would you like to come in?" Nora asked. "I can make tea. Or decaf."

A prudent man would go. A wise man would avoid a situation rife with dangerous possibilities. The problem was that Caine had never thought of himself as either a wise or prudent man.

"Decaf sounds great. But you're tired and—"

"It's instant."

His last excuse gone, Caine said, "Perfect."

He followed her into the kitchen and sat at the table, watching her fill the kettle with water.

The trestle table was piled high with books and papers. One particular stack of typed pages caught his attention.

"What's this?"

When she saw what he was holding in his hands, she flushed. "Oh, just an article I've been working on."

He scanned the opening paragraphs. "It's about treating children in emergency rooms?"

"Trauma centers," Nora corrected. "Emergency rooms are too geared to nonsurgical emergencies, like asthma, dehydration, stomach pumping, things like that. Which means they function just fine ninety-eight percent of the time.

"Until a trauma victim shows up. And things become even more complicated when the victim is a child."

"Like Dylan."

He lifted his gaze from the paper; his eyes met hers, asking her to finally share the most tragic experience of their lives with him.

Knowing what he needed and needing it, too, Nora didn't take her eyes away. "Yes," she said softly. "Like Dylan." She took a deep breath. "There's something I've been wanting to say." The teakettle began to whistle shrilly. Caine watched and waited as she poured the water over the dark crystals. She sat down across from him.

"When I stopped by to check on Maggie yesterday," she said quietly, "Devlin told me that you still blame yourself for Dylan's death."

When Caine's grandfather had divulged that particular piece of intimate information, Nora had been shocked.

"I think that's when I finally realized that it was time for me to stop blaming you. And for you to stop blaming yourself."

"Oh, hell, Nora, if Dylan hadn't been in the car—"

"You're being too hard on yourself." How strange that after all the years of blaming Caine for the death of their child, she now wanted so desperately to convince him of the contrary.

"I had a teammate in Detroit," Caine said slowly, painfully. "A shortstop. He dabbled in a lot of Eastern religions. When I knew him, he was into Zen.

"Used to drive us crazy, sitting stark-naked in front of his locker before every game, chanting his mantra. But I have to admit, he was the best player under pressure I've ever seen.

"One time, on a road trip, he told me something I've never forgotten."

"What's that?"

"He said that there is no such thing as coincidence, that life is only a response to Karma. That every word we utter, every breath we take, stirs the cosmos around us. That around every corner is a consequence, under every rock a repercussion."

Nora rose abruptly from the table and began to open a box of cookies. "I refuse to believe that Dylan's death was part of some enormous cosmic plan."

"But how do you know he's not right? What if it was a consequence of my ambition?" Caine asked. "How else can you explain that he died the day after I learned I was finally getting called up to the majors?"

"Coincidence, dammit!" Her hands were trembling as she overturned the box, scattering cookies all over the table. "I was just as ambitious as you, Caine. We were both obsessed by our own goals.

"But that doesn't mean that we didn't love our son. And it certainly doesn't mean that either of us caused his death. It was an accident. A stupid, tragic, senseless accident."

The words were meant to comfort Caine. What Nora hadn't expected was, that for the first time in nine years, she could truly believe them.

"You sound awfully sure of that."

Nora drew in a long, shuddering breath. "I've seen too many children die since that day. I've had a great deal of time to think about how that could happen and why."

"Which brings us back to this paper."

"Yes." She took another breath, clearing her mind. "There are so many things people need to know about the treatment of children who've suffered accidents. So many ways they're different from adults."

"Such as?"

"Well, a child's head is much larger, in relation to the rest of his body, than an adult's. Which makes him more vulnerable to head injuries.

"And then there's his spleen. When an injured adult comes into the emergency room with a bleeding spleen, it's standard procedure to remove it. An adult will never miss it. But to a child, the spleen is vital to the immune system.

"If you take it out, the patient will seem to recover. Until he catches a cold or the flu, and since his body can't handle the infection, he dies from what should have been a simple case of the sniffles."

She frowned, remembering the first time she'd encountered such a case. A light case of flu that should have been cured with chicken soup, fluids and a few days spent in bed watching cartoons had killed a six-year-old former accident victim.

"And bones," she said. "Children's bones have a remarkable ability to heal themselves, but the problem is that broken bones grow faster than unbroken ones, so if you set a child's leg the same way you do an adult's, the broken leg will grow longer than the other.

"So many things," she murmured, glancing down at the papers he was still holding.

"Sounds like too many for a mere paper," Caine observed. "Perhaps you ought to write a book."

"And while I'm at it, I might as well shoot for the moon and establish a pediatric trauma center in my spare time," she said. "All I'd have to do is give up sleep."

Having watched her grueling schedule, Caine knew she was right. "Too bad. It sounds like a book that needs to be written."

Nora nodded an agreement.

When the grandfather clock in the foyer struck the hour, Caine glanced down at his watch in surprise. "It'll be daylight soon. You're going to be beat."

"It's my monthly Saturday off," Nora reminded him. "I can sleep all day."

Caine found the idea of spending a rainy Saturday in bed with this woman infinitely appealing.

"Well, I'd better get going and let you get some rest." Even as he pushed himself away from the table, Caine wished she would ask him to stay.

A very strong part of Nora did not want Caine to leave. Telling herself that it was for the best, she stood, as well.

"Thanks again," she said, walking him to the door. "For everything."

"Thank you," he replied. "For the coffee, and the cookies and, well, everything."

Knowing Nora no longer blamed him for Dylan's death had taken a very heavy load from Caine's shoulders. If she could forgive him, perhaps he could learn to forgive himself.

They stood in the foyer, inches apart, looking at each other. Caine brushed his knuckles down her cheek. It felt too damn good for comfort.

"Sleep tight." Caine watched the desire rise in her remarkable eyes and knew he should go. Now, before it was too late.

"You, too. Give Maggie my love."

"I'll do that. See you on Monday. So you can take out my stitches," he said, reminding her of his new appointment date.

Because he wanted to kiss her, wanted to drag her upstairs to the bedroom and discover exactly how much of her elusive scent remained on her warm skin, Caine turned and trotted down the steps to the car parked at the curb.

Nora opened her mouth to call him back, then closed it. But she did remain standing in the open doorway until the Ferrari's taillights had disappeared around the corner.

Later that day, Caine flew a pair of tourists from California to Orcas Island. Since the honeymooning couple was clearly besotted with one another, he doubted they fully appreciated the magnificent scenery.

Sunday he spent up to his elbows in soapsuds. Imbued with a new sense of purpose, he scrubbed the cabin floor, scoured the countertops and evicted the spiders that had taken up residence in the high ceiling corners. While washing the front window, he watched a robin weave a scarlet ribbon into the nest the robin was energetically building in a nearby tree and felt a strange sort of kinship with the red-breasted bird.

On Monday morning, the cabin was clean enough for his mother to visit. After a trip to the dump, where the circling sea gulls seemed delighted with his nearly three weeks' collection of trash, Caine returned home, sat down at the kitchen table with a pot of coffee and a legal pad and began making telephone calls to friends and sports contacts around the country.

By the time he left for his appointment with Nora, Caine felt, for the first time in a very long while, that he finally had his life back on track.

Spring light latticed the landscape with shifting shades of green: the goldish green of early willows bent along the streams, the reddish green of maple leaves unfolding from their burst buds, the delicate green of bracken fern uncurling slender fronds, and always, the deep blue-green of water.

Caine had long ago decided that there were probably more shades of green on Washington's Olympic Peninsula than his Irish ancestors could have counted in Eire. During his years away from the peninsula, he'd grown increasingly homesick for such sights.

But as he drove to the clinic, the willows, the maple leaves, the ferns and the water all went unnoticed. Because the only thing he could see was Nora's exquisite face.

As was usual on Mondays, a continuous stream of patients filed into Nora's clinic. Fortunately Kirstin, her nurse, had returned from maternity leave and things were running a great deal more smoothly.

Nora finished wrapping Eva Nelson's sprained ankle. The teenager had stumbled while backpacking. Warning Eva to keep any stress off the ankle until the sprain was healed, to keep the leg elevated as much as possible, and to take aspirin as needed, Nora walked her to the reception area. That's when she saw Caine, sprawled in her grandmother's Queen Anne chair as if he belonged there. With his long legs stretched out in front of him, he seemed to take up half the narrow foyer.

"Good afternoon, Mr. O'Halloran," she greeted him formally.

"Afternoon, Doc."

"I can see you now."

It did not escape Nora's notice that her very efficient nurse, who was watching Caine surreptitiously as she filled out an insurance receipt for the injured teenager, made an uncharacteristic mistake, voided the form with a murmured apology to the patient and had to begin again.

"You've no idea how much I appreciate your making time for me in your busy schedule," he drawled, rising to follow her back into the room in his easy, loose-hipped athlete's gait.

"Get up on the table—"

"I know the drill, Nora." He grinned. "Want me to take off my clothes again?"

"That isn't necessary." She turned and reached into the cabinet for surgical scissors and gloves.

Her sharp tone pleased him. Caine had noticed long ago that very few things got under Nora's skin. He decided the fact that he was one of them was definitely an encouraging sign.

When Nora turned around he was standing behind her, closer than she'd thought.

"Did you have a nice weekend?" he asked.

"Lovely," she replied. "And you?"

"Actually I did. I flew another one of Maggie's charters to the islands. It felt funny being paid to do something I'd do for free. Funny, but nice."

"You always said you'd play ball for free."

"Got me there," Caine said agreeably. Not quite ready to fill her in on what else he'd been doing, he pulled himself up onto the table, dangled his legs and said, "Snip away, Doc. I'm ready."

"I received a call from the hospice coordinator today about Maggie," she said conversationally as she clipped the first stitch with deft hands.

"I know." Caine felt a slight tug against his scalp. "We made a deal."

"What kind of deal?" *Clip.* Another stitch gone.

"In return for her entering the hospice program, I promised to quit drinking too much, stop speeding, and turn celibate."

"I can't imagine Maggie holding you to that last one." *Clip. Clip. Snip. Snip.*

"You're right." There was a sudden charge in the air as his gaze met hers. "She pointed out, in her inimitably direct way, that it wasn't right, my courting one woman while I was technically married to another. So I promised to stay away from you until my divorce is final. Which makes celibacy a given."

His stormy eyes lowered slowly, purposefully to her lips, the look as physical as a kiss, and lingered there for a long, heartfelt moment. "Since you're the only woman I want."

Her lovely face was a contradiction of emotions. Caine saw anxiety, fear, irritation, and most encouraging of all, need. "Back off, Caine."

"I told you, that's exactly what I'm going to do," he agreed with an easy smile. "For now."

He wanted to draw her into his arms and resisted the urge. "Haven't you noticed that I've been in your office for at least ten minutes without giving in to the impulse to kiss you?"

"Dammit, Caine—"

"May I ask a question?"

She peeled off the thin gloves. "I suppose that depends on the question."

"Are we done?"

"Taking out the stitches? Yes."

"Then the professional part of this visit is over?"

"Yes." Her voice wasn't quite as strong as before.

"Good."

With a silent apology to his grandmother, Caine slid off the table, put his arms around Nora, lowered his mouth to hers and kissed her with all the pent-up passion he'd been feeling.

"We can't keep doing this," she complained weakly when the long, hot kiss finally ended.

His lips plucked enticingly at hers. "Give me one good reason to stop."

"How about your wife?"

"Bull's-eye." Sighing, Caine reluctantly released her. "I hate it when you insist on acting like a grown-up."

"One of us has to." Her cheeks were still flushed, her lips swollen, and her eyes were laced with desire. "Perhaps it'd be better if we just stayed away from one another."

"In this town?" Caine knew that no matter where they were living, things had gone too far to back away now.

"You have a point," Nora conceded reluctantly. "I suppose I'll be seeing you next Friday night."

Midsummer's Eve was an annual festival dating back to the days of Swedish pagan worship, a celebration of the summer solstice. Years ago someone had gotten the idea to add a contest of lumbering skills to the festivities, which resulted in loggers coming from all over the country to try to win the purse that had grown larger each year. Neither Caine nor Nora had attended since the night Dylan had been conceived.

"I suppose. If I'm in town."

"Oh. Are you taking another charter for Maggie?" she asked with more casualness than she was feeling.

"No." He'd been trying to think of a way to break the news. "I got a call from the Tigers."

"Oh? I hadn't realized you'd recovered well enough to pitch again."

Caine watched her shutting up, like a wildflower closing its petals prior to a storm. "I haven't. They're about to fire their pitching coach and I'm on the short list to be his replacement."

"I see." She did, all too well. "Does that mean you've given up the idea of playing again?"

"For the time being." He flexed his fingers. "Hell, there's no point in trying to fool myself any longer, Nora. I've still got the moves, but I've lost the feeling necessary for absolute control."

"Well, then, I certainly wish you luck with this new offer."

The intimacy between them was gone, replaced by that cold formality Caine had always hated. Only the knowledge that Nora was iciest when she was experiencing the greatest inner turmoil kept him from pushing.

"Thanks. These days I need all the luck I can get."

He decided to leave before they got into an argument regarding what she'd always considered his self-centered career choices. "You don't have to see me out." He bent his head, stealing another quick kiss. "I know the way."

Frustrated by the way he could still cause such havoc to her emotional equilibrium, Nora curved her fingers around the handle of the surgical scissors. She was unreasonably tempted to throw them at his cocky, sun-streaked head.

Instead, she deliberately put them down on the table, closed her eyes and struggled for calm—something that was difficult to achieve when she heard Caine's deep voice, followed by an all-too-familiar rumbling chuckle coming from the foyer.

If she was upset by the way Caine had left her shaken—and, dammit, wanting—Nora was appalled at the surge of dark jealousy caused by the sound of Kirstin's appreciative, answering laugh.

As IF ANCIENT pagan gods had benevolently conspired with Mother Nature, Midsummer Eve was warm and clear. A full moon hung like a silver dollar in the sky, bathing the town in a light that was nearly as bright as day, only softer.

Japanese lanterns had been strung around the square; white lights twinkled in the broad leaves of maple trees planted by some long-ago town council. At one end of the square, men drank beer from a keg and slung horseshoes. The plink of forged iron shoes against the iron stakes joined with the sound of crickets.

Tables were covered with food: cold fruit soups, a variety of local clams and oysters, *pyttipanna*—a traditional late-supper hash—and platters of salmon topped with *senapssas*, a cold mustard-dill sauce.

On the dessert table, delicate *plättar*—traditional Swedish pancakes topped with lingonberries—shared space with blueberry filled tortes topped with a frothy meringue and *mazarintorta*—a raspberry torte topped with lemon icing. At the end of the dessert table was hot *punsch*, a lethal brandy-and-rum drink. If all that weren't enough to satiate appetites, people stood in line, paper plates in hand, waiting for one of the flame-broiled Olympic burgers Ingrid Johansson was cooking on an enormous charcoal grill.

The opposite end of the square had been turned into a

modern-day Highland games, where loggers competed to win the coveted purse that this year had grown to five thousand dollars. There was the angry, beelike drone of chain saws, the thwack of an ax landing on target, raucous laughter and wild splashing whenever a hapless logger tumbled off a rolling log into the fishpond.

On her way across the green, Nora paused to watch the women's ax-throwing contest.

"Now that's a magnificent, if admittedly frightening sight," a deep voice murmured in her ear. "A beautiful woman swinging a double-headed ax."

She turned around, struggled to keep the smile off her face, and failed. "Hi."

Caine would have had to be deaf not to hear the uncensored pleasure in her voice. "Hi, yourself."

She was wearing something floaty and flowery and very feminine. She smelled like a spring garden. He reached out and fingered a dangling earring crafted from pastel shells. "You look absolutely gorgeous."

Color stained her cheeks. "Thank you."

The billowy skirt ended well below her knees; until tonight, Caine had never realized exactly how sexy a woman's calves could be.

"The town council made a big mistake." He was looking down at her as if he wanted to grab her by the hair and drag her off to his cave. Nora looked up at him as if she hoped he would.

"A mistake?" She glanced around at the festival that was an obvious success. "About what?"

"They should have voted you Queen. Instead of Britta Nelson."

Nora followed his gaze to the *majstång*—the flower-decked pole that a circle of young girls were currently dancing around. Fifteen-year-old Britta Nelson was wearing her crown, a circlet of fresh flowers, perched atop her silvery blond hair.

"I brought you something." Caine pulled a bouquet of wildflowers from behind his back.

"Oh, they're lovely." In spite of her better judgment, Nora buried her nose in the fragrant blooms.

"There are seven different kinds."

The significance of that number did not escape her. Swedish folklore decreed any maiden who placed seven different wildflowers beneath her pillow on Midsummer Eve would dream of the man she would marry.

"Really, Caine..."

When she would have backed away, he captured her hand and lifted it to his lips. "Don't tell me you're afraid you'll dream about me?"

"Of course not."

"I've been dreaming about you." Smiling, he began to kiss her fingers. "Every night. Want to hear a few of the more interesting ones?"

When his lips moved to the soft skin at the center of her palm, although Nora the doctor knew it was impossible, Nora the woman could have sworn that every muscle in her body began to melt. Knowing that nothing in Tribulation went unnoticed, she yanked her hand free.

"No." She put her hands behind her back to keep them out of Caine's range. Unfortunately, such defensive behavior made it impossible to push him away when he proceeded to back her up against the trunk of the maple tree behind her. "I don't."

"Too bad." He put his hands on either side of her head, effectively holding her hostage. "My favorite is the one where we're flying over the ocean in Maggie's Learjet—"

"Maggie doesn't have a Learjet—"

"It's a dream," Caine argued easily. "Anyway, we're

over the ocean, and all we can see for miles in all directions, is the blue-green of the sea and the blue of the sky. It's as if we're the only two people in the world.

"Just you and me and the wild blue yonder. And here's where the good part begins: I put the plane on autopilot, and—"

There was the sound of a throat clearing behind them.

"Ah, excuse me, Caine. Hi, Nora," Joe Bob Carroll said apologetically. "Sorry to interrupt. But your grandpappy's lookin' for the both of you, Caine. Since he looked a little ragged around the edges, I told him to wait over by the horseshoe pits while I went and found you."

Caine dropped his hands to his sides. He gave Nora a worried look. "Devlin stayed home with Maggie tonight. If he left her to come here..."

Nora wanted to cover his grimly set lips with her own, to press kisses all over that dark, tortured face. She longed to tell him that there was no need to worry, that his grandmother would live to be a hundred.

In the end, she merely lifted a palm to his cheek.

"We'd better go see what he wants," she said in the quiet, reassuring tone she'd adopted during her years of medical practice.

Nora took her ex-husband's hand in hers and led him, atypically meek as a lamb, across the crowded green, through the throng of merrymakers, toward Devlin O'Halloran.

WHEN THEY REACHED THE house, Ellen and Mike O'Halloran were waiting. Mike, Caine's father, had always been a taciturn man, more comfortable with his lures and lines than with people. A crisis did not change his nature.

After murmuring a vague, inarticulate greeting to

Nora, he gave her an awkward hug. Although he might not be as talkative as either Devlin or Caine, the painful prospect of losing his mother had made his dark eyes moist.

Ellen O'Halloran's face, still remarkably unlined for a woman nearing sixty, was tanned to a deep hazelnut color from the life-style change that now had her spending so much of her time outdoors. Her short hair was the color of autumn leaves, laced with random streaks of sun-lightened auburn and silver.

As she embraced her former mother-in-law, Nora experienced a moment's confusion over whether she was here in her role as doctor or family.

As a doctor, although she continually fought against it, death had become a fellow traveler, at times welcome, most often not. As a family member—at the moment, her divorce from Caine seemed inconsequential—Nora shared everyone's feelings of helplessness and sorrow.

The hospice nurse came out of the bedroom and drew Nora aside. "I informed Maggie's family that she won't last the night," she murmured. "But, of course, I've been wrong before."

Nora knew only too well the futility of second-guessing death. "I'd better examine her."

Maggie was asleep when Nora entered the bedroom. She was wearing an old-fashioned ivory cotton gown with long sleeves trimmed with hand-tatted lace. Her thinning red hair was spread across the embroidered pillow like strands of silver touched by a setting sun. Her face, in repose, was calm.

Nora reached down and lifted a frail wrist. Her pulse was thin and thready. Nora had just lowered the elderly woman's hand to the sheet again when Maggie's blue eyes popped open.

"I figured that was you," she said. "Caine always said you smelled like wildflowers after a spring rain." Maggie laced their fingers together. "He's right."

"Speaking of Caine," Nora said, "he's waiting to see you."

"I know. I've already said my goodbyes to Michael and Ellen and was just hangin' on until you and Caine got here." Her eyes fluttered shut. Nora slid her thumb to Maggie's wrist and was relieved to find her pulse unchanged. A few moments later, Maggie's eyes opened again. "So how was the festival?"

"Nice." Nora knew Maggie wanted particulars so she filled her in on the sawdust competition, the dancing, the Japanese lanterns, and the smorgasbord.

"Did Eva Magnuson bring her apple torte?"

"Of course."

"Her apples are never tart enough," Maggie complained. "And her crust is like concrete. But she's been makin' the damn thing forever, so no one has the heart to tell her.

"I remember Midsummer Eve back during the war," Maggie mused. "We couldn't have the lanterns because of the blackouts. Never knew when a Japanese submarine was going to come steaming up the strait to the shipyards."

She closed her eyes again. The corners of her mouth twitched upward. "A lot of smooching went on in the shadows behind those old maples, let me tell you. Especially with all the boys shippin' out. Nothin' like a war to steam up a romance."

The smile faded. "Michael's hurtin' bad," Maggie continued. "Not that he'd ever admit it. If I lived another eighty-two years, I'd probably never figure out how a magpie like me could've given birth to such a close-mouthed boy.

"But he's got Ellen, so I'm not worried about him. Of course, poor Caine's probably gonna carry on something awful because he couldn't keep his grandmother alive."

She sighed, pressed a hand against her failing heart and took a ragged breath. "Caine always did take too much on his own shoulders. But it's the boy's nature, so what can you do?"

Maggie's lashes drifted down again, but she didn't fall asleep. "Caine's been telling me about this teammate of his. Some Buddhist fella. They believe in reincarnation."

"The Detroit shortstop," Nora remembered.

"I've been thinking about that a lot, lately," Maggie admitted. "I kinda like the idea of comin' back again. Maybe this time as an astronaut."

"The first woman to pilot a spaceship to Mars," Nora suggested with a smile.

Maggie smiled, as well. "I'd like that. Devlin wouldn't. He gets airsick." She chuckled again. "Imagine, a man who's spent most of his life on the water getting airsick. I never have been able to figure that one out."

She drifted off again. Nora had just about decided that it was time to bring the family in when Maggie opened her eyes, fixed her with her bright blue gaze and said, "If there does turn out to be a heaven, I'll tell Dylan his mama says hello."

Nora had to swallow past the lump in her throat. "Thank you."

"If we do get to come back again, I reckon your paths will cross one of these days and you can tell him yourself," Maggie decided.

Tears were burning at the backs of her lids. Nora could only nod.

"You'd better send Caine in now, Nora. After you give me a kiss."

Nora bent her head and brushed her lips against the older woman's cheek. Her skin was as thin and dry as old parchment.

"I love you, Maggie." All right, perhaps it wasn't the most professional thing to say, but it was the truth.

"And I love you, girl." It took an obvious effort, but Maggie managed to lift her hand from the sheet to pat Nora's cheek. "Take good care of my grandson," she whispered. "I know he can be a bit of a hotshot from time to time, Nora, but he's a good boy. Deep down."

"I know." That, too, was the truth.

It was with a heavy heart that Nora went to the door and gestured toward Caine. When he entered the bedroom, she brushed her fingers against his rigid jaw, then left him alone with his grandmother.

He'd been watching Maggie's decline for weeks, but in the back of his mind, Caine had refused to accept the fact that his grandmother was dying. Even now, looking at her ivory complexion and her frail frame, he couldn't face the sad truth.

"You're missing the dancing."

"I know. And that really gets my goat. Your pappy's a good dancer." A faint reminiscent light flickered in Maggie's eyes.

"The first time we danced together was on Midsummer Eve. I'd landed in town as part of a five-girl flying exhibition team. The town council hired us thinkin' we might bring some tourists in from the cities. Your pappy was mayor. It was his idea."

Caine sat down in the straight-backed chair beside the bed. "Did you? Bring in more tourists?"

Maggie shrugged her frail shoulders. "Don't remember. Only thing I recollect about that night is dancin' the rumba with Devlin. After that, everything kinda passed in a blur. The next day, when the sun came up, the rest of the girls moved on."

"But you stayed." It was one of Caine's favorite stories.

"And never regretted a single day. What your pappy and I had was special. We both knew that right off the bat." Maggie's eyes closed, but her hand reached across the sheets to pat his.

"It's taken you and Nora a little longer, but you'll get there. Eventually. Like that Buddhist friend of yours says, a man can't escape his Karma.... Would you do me a favor?"

"You've got it," Caine said without hesitation.

"Would you help me brush my hair?"

She was as light as a feather; Caine lifted her with ease and propped her up against the plump goose-down pillows. Retrieving a silver-handled hairbrush, he began stroking the brush over her scalp, smoothing out the once-fiery strands.

"Mmm," Maggie murmured. "That feels good." Just when Caine thought she'd fallen asleep, Maggie said, "Love's a powerful thing, Caine. Even more powerful than fate. And you and Nora have got both goin' for you."

He'd come to that same realization himself. Now all he had to do was convince Nora. "I know, Gram. And that's why you have to stay well enough to stick around for the wedding."

"There's nothin' I'd like better. But don't you worry, boy, I'll be there in spirit." Caine watched her struggle to lift her lids. "How do I look?"

"Beautiful." On impulse, he spritzed her with the lilac cologne she'd always worn. "You smell pretty good, too.

If you weren't my grandmother, I'd probably have to give pappy a run for his money."

She dimpled at that, looking remarkably, for one fleeting second, like a girl of sixteen. "You and Devlin," she murmured. "Two peas in a pod. Both of you must've kissed the blarney stone in some past life."

She smoothed her hair with a trembling hand and pinched her cheeks. "Speakin' of your pappy," she said, "I think you'd better send him in."

"Gram..."

"It's my time, Caine," Maggie said soothingly. "And as much as I do truly love you, I still need to say goodbye to the best rumba dancer in Tribulation."

Caine no longer attempted to check his tears. They flowed down his face, onto the sheets, and splashed on his grandmother's blue-veined hand. He wanted to drag her into his arms and beg her not to die, but since she looked as breakable as a piece of fine porcelain, he forced himself to simply press a kiss against the top of her freshly brushed hair.

"God, I love you," he said in a choked voice. Then, before he lost it completely, he turned and walked toward the door that his grandfather had already opened, as if answering some unspoken call.

Devlin patted Caine on the shoulder, then squared his own broad shoulders and crossed the room, forgoing the chair to sit on the edge of the bed.

"You are still the most gorgeous girl in Tribulation," he said, running a hand down her hair.

Rather than accuse him of exaggerating, as she had Caine, Maggie turned her head and pressed her dry lips against his palm. "And you're still the handsomest man."

He stretched out beside her, drew her close and knew he'd never see a lilac bush without thinking of Maggie.

They stayed that way for a long, silent time, her head on his shoulder, his lips against the top of her head.

"I love you, Margaret Rose Murphy O'Halloran," Devlin whispered after a time.

"And I love you, Devlin Patrick O'Halloran." She tilted her head to smile up at him, but her eyes were earnest. "I want you to promise me something."

"Anything."

"Just in case that shortstop friend of Caine's is right, and some day, in some other life, you meet a woman—maybe an aviatrix or even an astronaut—who asks you to rumba, promise me that you'll say yes."

"I promise." He touched his lips to hers and covered her breast with his broad hand. "Yes. Always."

Devlin felt the quick flutter of her heart, like that of a wounded sparrow, against his fingertips. Then it was still. The light outside the window turned from ebony to gray to a pale, misty silver. Pink fingers of dawn began creeping into the room.

And still Devlin remained, with his bride, the light of his life for more than half a century, in his arms.

Remembering.

12

THE MEMORIAL SERVICE for Maggie was held, at her request, at the airport. Hundreds came to pay tribute to the woman who'd brought so much life and laughter and spirit to Tribulation.

The mourners who overflowed the tent stood beneath black umbrellas, until finally, when the drizzle escalated into a downpour, the services were moved inside the hangar.

When the rain stopped and the pewter clouds parted, Caine and Devlin—the older man fortified by the Dramamine tablet Nora had given him—took off in Maggie's beloved Cessna to spread her ashes over the mountain meadows she'd loved.

The others retired to Mike and Ellen's, where they shared a potluck supper and swapped Maggie stories, each more outrageous than the last, all of them true.

It was late when Nora returned home, but she wasn't surprised to see Caine sitting on the porch in the wicker swing, waiting for her. Neither was she surprised by the surge of pure pleasure that flowed through her.

"Hi." She slipped her hands into the skirt pockets of her black dress. "How's Devlin?"

"About as well as can be expected," Caine replied. "I offered to take him back to the cabin with me, but he wanted to stay at the house. He says he can feel Maggie's spirit there."

"I suppose that's not surprising."

"I guess not." Caine raked his hands through his hair. "He feels she's hanging around to make sure he's okay with all this."

"That's not surprising, either. Are you?"

"Am I what?"

"Okay with all this?"

Caine shrugged. "I suppose. As much as I can be.... By the way, I got a call today from my lawyer. By this time tomorrow, I'll be a free man."

Her heart soared, even as Nora attempted to bank her joy. "I guess congratulations are in order." Wicker creaked as she sat down beside him.

"Thanks. The entire process looked like it was going to last until the next century, so I decided to make an end run around the legal eagles and wrote out a generous enough check to send her to the Dominican Republic."

"That's football," Nora murmured.

"What?"

"An end run. That's football."

He chuckled. "I can remember when you thought a tight end was a groupie in too-snug jeans."

"I've been working in a man's profession," she reminded. "You can't escape sports talk in the doctors' lounge."

"I thought doctors only talked about golf."

"I suppose they do, mostly."

"Did you ever take it up so you'd have something to do on Wednesday afternoons?"

"Golf? No." Nora shook her head. "I never could figure out whether to hit the ball when the dragon's mouth was open or closed."

He laughed and put his arm around her. Nora didn't move away. For a while there was only the soft sigh of the night breeze in the trees and a swish-swish sound as they swung gently.

"Was it hard?" she asked finally. "Scattering Maggie's ashes?"

"I thought it would be," Caine admitted. "But the meadows were in full bloom and while we were circling, looking for a space, a ray of sun came out of the clouds, and gilded this one spot on the mountainside pure gold. I looked at Devlin and he looked at me, and we both knew that somehow, Maggie was guiding us."

"She probably was," Nora said quietly. "I worried when you didn't show up at the potluck."

"Devlin just wanted to go home. After I dropped him off, I drove to Port Angeles and played a little catch with Johnny."

"That was nice of you."

"I did it more for myself than for him. I like the kid. A lot."

"And he idolizes you. How's he doing?"

"Okay." Caine shrugged. "He's worried that no one will adopt him because people would rather have a new baby."

"Most people would, I suppose. But Johnny's a wonderful little boy. He'll find a family."

"That's what I told him," Caine agreed.

They fell silent again. Somewhere in a distant treetop an owl hooted.

"I brought you something," Caine said.

When he reached into his pocket, Nora thought he was going to give her some small memento of his grandmother, but instead, he handed her a legal-size white envelope.

Slanting him a questioning look, she slid her fingernail under the flap and opened it. "A check?"

The moon was riding high above the horizon, the cool white light bright enough to enable Nora to read the amount. "I don't understand."

Stunned, unable to believe what her eyes were telling her, she slowly counted all the zeros again. "It's made out to the Dylan Anderson O'Halloran Memorial Pediatric Trauma Center."

Caine nodded. "That's right."

"But there isn't any such center."

"Not now. But there will be."

She couldn't believe he was serious. Her first thought was that this was some sort of grandstand play to win her approval. Her second thought was that Caine was not the type of man to indulge in such subterfuge.

She stood and began to pace. "But a trauma center is so very expensive."

"Tiffany didn't get all my money, Nora."

"But even you can't fund it by yourself."

"I know that. But I'm a helluva fund-raiser. You should hear my after-dinner speeches. Besides, I'm going to have help."

She stopped in her tracks. "What kind of help?"

"There's going to be an All-Star baseball game in October, after the World Series and before winter ball begins in South America," he informed her. "All proceeds going to the center. ESPN has committed to broadcasting the game and here's a list of people who've signed up to play. I expect more when the word gets out."

Nora scanned the list he'd pulled from his pocket. The names represented the top stars, past and present, of the game.

"You've been busy."

Caine shrugged. "I spent the past few weeks making some phone calls. It kept me out of the pool halls."

He'd done more than make phone calls. It was obvious that he'd spent a great deal of time and effort on the project. Not to mention money. "I can't let you do this."

"It's too late to stop me, Nora. Besides, I'm not doing it for you," Caine argued calmly. "I'm doing it for all the little kids like Dylan who need a fighting chance."

Caine's incredible plans left Nora feeling drained. She sat back in the swing and stared up at the star-spangled sky.

"After all these years, I didn't think there was anything you could do to surprise me," she said finally. "But you've succeeded."

"I'm glad to hear that. But I didn't do it as some elaborate scheme to get you back in my life, Nora."

"I know."

They resumed swinging.

Need was a fist, twisting at Caine's gut, crawling beneath his skin, burning him from the inside out. With effort, he pushed it down.

As if reading his mind, Nora turned her head so that her face was inches from Caine's. His arm was stretched along the top of the swing; the slightest movement would have it around her shoulders.

"I guess I'd better go home," he said quietly. "Before I stoop to begging."

When he began to rise—fully, honorably, intending to leave—she placed her hand on his arm. Her eyes, more gold than brown in the streaming moonlight, revealed her own desire.

"You wouldn't have to beg."

He couldn't resist. He had to touch her, if only to cup her face with his hand. "I want you to be sure about this, Nora. Very sure."

"I am." Her answering laugh was as quick and shaky as

her pulse. "In fact, I don't think I've ever been so sure about anything in my life."

She slid her arms around his neck, her smile a seduction in itself. If Scheherazade had flashed that fatal, womanly smile at the Sultan, Caine mused, she definitely wouldn't have needed to tell the guy stories to keep him interested during those thousand and one nights.

"Kiss me, Caine." Nora's soft voice curled around him like smoke. "Kiss me the way you were going to kiss me at the festival."

He combed his hands through her hair, gathering it into a knot at the nape of her neck, and held her gaze to his. "If I do," he warned, "it won't stop with a kiss."

"Good." Her fingers were playing with the curls at the back of his collar. "Because I want you to make love to me." Her eyes were open and fixed on his. "Nobody has ever made me fly so high."

Caine hadn't come to Nora's house to take her to bed. He'd only wanted to be with her, to tell her about the center, and, perhaps, ease the pain of losing his grandmother just a little.

He thought of his promise to Maggie, to stay away from Nora until he was free.

But dammit, Tiffany was on her way to the Dominican Republic—along with a cashier's check for one million dollars—and in a matter of hours a marriage that should have been declared dead at the altar would be legally dissolved.

Reminding himself that he'd never been bucking for sainthood, Caine tangled his hands in her hair and kissed her—a deep, drugging kiss that had heat pouring out of him and into her.

Kissing Nora was like partaking of a feast after a long

fast. Hunger. Greed. Need. They rose like ancient demons, battering at his insides.

Fighting for patience, Caine buried his lips in the soft scent of her hair. Every ragged breath he took was an agony of effort.

"I want to make love with you, too, sweetheart." He ran his palms down her arms and struggled valiantly for some semblance of control. "But let's try to keep this flight from being over too fast."

"I'll try if you will. But I've never had a great deal of self-control where you're concerned, Caine."

"I know the feeling." Caine laced their fingers together and stood, bringing her to her feet with him.

When he led her into the house and up the stairs, Nora experienced a moment's hesitation—one that did not go unnoticed by Caine.

He stopped on the landing and framed her face between his hands. "If this isn't what you want—"

"It is." She pressed her lips against his quickly, cutting him off. Although she was thirty-two years old, there was no artifice in her kiss, no clever experience; only honest, feminine need.

"I've never wanted anyone the way I want you right now, Caine," she whispered when the brief flare ended. "I've never needed anyone the way I need you at this moment."

It was all he needed to hear. Holding hands again, they walked the rest of the way up the stairs and into her bedroom.

The room was a direct contrast to the proper, professional image Nora showed the world. It was pretty and feminine and smelled of flowers. It was the kind of room a man would only feel comfortable in if invited.

Antique perfume bottles stood atop her dresser along

with a trio of fat white candles and a dish of potpourri made from the petals of the scarlet roses Nora's grandmother had planted behind the house.

Framed photos, of friends and family, covered most of the rest of the dresser top.

Caine smiled when he saw a picture of Maggie, standing in front of a red Stinson four-seater she'd owned back in the 1950s. She was grinning with the sheer confidence of a woman who had never let any obstacle stand in her way.

Caine's gaze moved to an open sandalwood box where a strand of polite pearls was hopelessly entangled with gold hoops, and a pair of discreet silver stud earrings rested on velvet beside a funky ceramic pin shaped like a gray whale.

Caine remembered the pin well; he'd bought it for Nora on impulse one April day when they'd taken a cranky, teething Dylan on a ferryboat ride to Orcas Island. He was moved and vastly encouraged by the fact that she'd kept it all these years.

The hand-carved bed was wide and tall; the four posters reached almost to the ceiling. The mattress was covered with a wedding-ring quilt from some Anderson bride's hope chest. Piled atop the quilt were dozens of pillows—too small to be useful for anything other than feminine ornamentation—covered in lace and satin and pretty floral-chintz prints.

Beside the bed, he was pleased to see, his wildflowers sat in a white china pitcher he remembered Anna Anderson pouring milk from. He plucked a petal and rubbed it between his thumb and forefinger, releasing a burst of sweet fragrance.

"I dreamed of you that night," Nora murmured. "On Midsummer Eve."

He'd known she would. Just as he had dreamed of her.

Centuries of folklore hovered in the perfumed air between them. "But I don't think it counts," she whispered, "because I've been dreaming of you every night since you came back to Tribulation."

The soft admission was more than he'd dared to hope for. "Every night?"

"Yes." The single word shuddered from between her lips on a soft sigh. "Every single one."

A fierce burst of primitive satisfaction surged through his veins. "Although I've never been a man to worry about setting the scene for romance, I wanted to do this right." His gaze moved lingeringly over her face; he was making love to her with his eyes. "I had it all planned: champagne and red roses and music."

"I don't need champagne. Or roses. Or music." He was standing so close to her, Nora couldn't tell if it was Caine's heart beating so wildly, or her own. "All I need is you."

His eyes didn't waver from hers as he slowly traced the exquisite shape of her mouth with his thumb. His fingers explored the planes of her face and found her perfect. His mouth drank from hers with a gentleness he hadn't known he possessed.

When his tongue slipped between her parted lips to touch the tip of hers, Nora wondered how it was that her body could be so thrillingly alive while her mind remained so clouded.

Refusing to dwell on it, she let herself slide effortlessly into this seductive, misty world. She lifted her arms, entwined them around Caine's neck and pulled him to her. Their bodies fit just as she remembered. Perfectly. Wonderfully.

The more she gave, the more Caine wanted. He ached for her—body, mind and soul.

"All these years," he told her, "I've tried to forget the way you felt in my arms when we made love. And the incredible, terrifying way you make me feel."

"I know." She ran her fingers over his dark face. "I've tried to forget, too. And I've tried to pretend that it wasn't real—that it had been only a fantasy, a trick of memory."

The wonder of her admission shimmered in her voice. "But it was real." Her fingers moved down his neck, to the open collar of his shirt.

Something about Caine had always had Nora wanting to give him more than she'd given to any other man. Something about him always had her wanting more from him than any man had ever given her.

She pressed her lips against his warm skin, drinking in his mysterious male taste. "It's only ever been that way with you, Caine." Very slowly, he unbuttoned her dress. Caine O'Halloran had always made love the way he played baseball: with a skill that made every move seem eminently natural.

Yet, as his fingers fumbled with the small pearl buttons running down the front of her dress, he wondered why it was that this act, which he'd performed so many times before, could suddenly seem so different. So new. So frightening.

The buttons went all the way to the hem. Breathing a sigh of relief as he released the final one, Caine folded back the material. She was wearing a silk teddy with a low-cut lace-trimmed bodice and a pair of black, lace-topped thigh-high stockings that had looked appropriately somber with the dress, but now were incredibly sexy contrasted with the pale skin above them.

The fact that the teddy was as scarlet as sin made him

smile, reminding him of the first time he'd discovered her penchant for sexy lingerie.

When Caine slid the dress from her shoulders, Nora reached for him, but he caught her hands.

"No, let me." He brushed his lips against hers again, tempting, tantalizing, tormenting. "Let me see if I can make you float."

"You always could."

The crimson teddy smelled like her. Caine could have drowned in her scent. But since the temptation of her silky skin was even more irresistible, Caine dispensed with the sensual barrier. Slowly, thoroughly, he seduced her solely with his mouth. Her blood warmed, her pulse hummed. And then, as impossible as it sounded, Nora began to float.

She found herself lying on the bed without knowing how she'd gotten there. When Caine's lips closed around the rosy tip of her breast and tugged, Nora gasped; they moved on, scattering hot kisses over her stomach, the inside of her thigh, the back of her thigh, the back of her knee. His teeth nibbled at the ultrasensitive tendon that only he had ever discovered, creating a flash of heat that spiraled outward to her fingertips.

But she wasn't allowed to dwell on that riveting feeling. His mouth was everywhere, tasting, tempting its way along a seductive path from her tingling lips to her bare toes. Everywhere his lips touched, they left tormenting trails of heat. Her blood was molten, flowing hot and thick through her veins, then deeper still, to the bone.

Caine was a tender, but ruthless lover—driving her toward delirium as he turned her in his arms, bending her to his will, tasting every fragrant bit of exposed flesh. And just when Nora didn't think she could take any more, he drove her higher, to where the air grew thin and it became hard to breathe.

Dazzled, dazed, desperate, she closed her eyes and clung to him as the years peeled away. And then she was tumbling over the rocky precipice, shuddering as climax after impossible, breath-stealing climax slammed through her.

Caine watched Nora's dazed eyes fly open. He heard her astonishment as she gasped his name. Strangely, the absolute trust she'd shown him had made him feel like a hero again—for the first time in a very long while.

He held her until the wild, aching tremors passed.

"Lord, I've missed this," he murmured against her mouth. "I've missed you."

For what seemed like an eternity, Nora lay limp in his arms, her mind spinning, her heated skin drenched. How could she have forgotten that it was possible to feel so much?

Sometime during the heady lovemaking, Caine's clothes had vanished. But how could that be? When she couldn't remember a single instant when his lips or his hands had not been warming her body.

Outside the window, the large white moon rising in the sky made Caine's dark skin gleam. Nora touched his chest. His flesh under her stroking fingers was soft and smooth. But the muscle beneath was hard and wire-taut. She pressed her lips against that warm moist flesh, drinking in the texture, the taste, his earthy male scent.

She ran her hands over his body, delighting in the way his muscles rippled and clenched beneath her palm. She pressed her open mouth against his flat stomach and felt him shudder. She flicked her tongue over his pebbly dark nipple and heard him groan.

The idea that she could cause such a primitive response

was thrilling. Abandoning caution, she rose to her knees and ran her palms down his legs, her fingers exploring the corded muscles of his thighs, his calves. Testing, she touched her lips to the flesh her hands had warmed.

How had the tables turned so devastatingly? Caine wondered dizzily. Just moments ago, he'd been the one in absolute control. He'd been the one creating havoc with Nora's stunned senses.

But now, with just the delicate glide of her hands, the feel of her mouth against his skin, the scrape of her teeth against the aching flesh at the inside of his thigh, she was driving him beyond reason. Her daring touch was like a flame; his flesh burned with it.

Overcome with a heady feminine power, Nora laughed and trailed her tongue wetly down his chest. The throaty sound tolled in his head as his body throbbed. Frustration warred with passion. Caine wanted her to stop; he wanted her never to stop.

He ached to take her now, quickly, before she succeeded in making him mad, but his power was gone. Somehow, when he wasn't looking, Nora had stolen it; it had flowed from him into her and for the first time in his life, Caine was experiencing true helplessness.

Moaning her name between short ragged breaths, he reached for her, but his touch was vague, almost dream-like.

"Not yet," she whispered silkily.

He knew what she was going to do; every atom in his body was poised for that incredible moment when she would take his swollen sex into her soft wet mouth.

As if determined to torment him as he had tormented her, Nora drew the moment out. Her tongue slid hotly along his length, making him groan as he thrust his lean hips off the mattress in a mute plea for fulfillment.

But still she made him wait. When her tongue encircled the plum-hued tip, Caine thought he was going to explode.

"No more." Need made his tone raw.

He grabbed hold of Nora's shoulders, turned her onto her back and levered himself over her. His eyes locked with hers. A promise, felt by both, sizzled between them.

He gripped her hips to pull her close, but Nora was already rising to meet him, to draw him in.

Caine slid into her, steel into silk. His hands linked with hers. Their fingers tightened.

Outside the window the white moon rose higher. And so did they.

"THAT," CAINE SAID when he could talk again, "was definitely worth waiting for."

"Mmm." Nora's head was on his chest; she pressed a kiss against his cooling flesh.

She was basking in a warm and satisfied glow and would have been more than happy to spend the rest of her days just lying in Caine's arms.

Even as common sense told her that that would be a remarkably impractical way to spend her life, the romantic side of her that this man had always been able to tap could think of nothing that would bring more pleasure. Caine ran a lazy finger down her spine. "Have I mentioned that you're still the most incredibly beautiful woman I've ever known?"

"Flatterer." His touch created a new flare of arousal that was as sharp as it was sweet.

"It's true." Smiling, he wound a thick strand of her hair around his hand. "And even now, after all we've shared, I still want you more than I've ever wanted any other woman."

"I want you, too," she admitted with a soft sigh.

He glanced down at her. "You don't sound very happy about that."

"It's just that nothing has changed." She was trembling. Caine felt an ominous feeling of foreboding and ignored it.

"Everything's changed." After brushing a kiss against the top of her head, he untangled himself from their embrace, left the bed and found his jeans.

"I have something for you."

"You've already given me so much," Nora protested, thinking of the generous check, not to mention all the work he'd been doing to establish her dream clinic. She sat up against the pillows.

"That was business. This is strictly personal."

Nora froze when he handed her the familiar blue sapphire set in antique gold filigree. "It's Maggie's engagement ring."

"Got it on the first try. She wanted you to have it."

"Me?"

Nora stared down at the ring, remembering that Devlin had bought his bride-to-be a sapphire, rather than a more traditional diamond, because it was the color of the sky she loved so well.

She ran her finger over the intricate gold weave. "You'd think Devlin would want to keep it."

"He and Maggie decided that it didn't make any sense to have it stashed away in some forgotten drawer."

"But—"

"They figured, and I agreed, that you might like it. And since we didn't exactly have a traditional wedding the first time around, I never got you a proper engagement ring."

"The first time?"

The mattress sighed as Caine sat down on the edge of the bed beside her. "You know how I feel, Nora. I love you. And, unless every instinct I've got has gone on the blink, you love me, too."

She couldn't lie any longer. Not to herself. Not to Caine. "I do."

"So the next logical thing to do is to get married."

"Caine—"

"In fact, the cabin's all ready for you to move in. I shoveled out the trash, washed the windows, changed the sheets and dusted. Even beneath the couch." He was more than a little pleased with himself about that. "And the refrigerator's filled with those healthy green vegetables you like."

"I'm sorry. But I can't marry you, Caine."

"Can't? Or won't?" Nora thought she detected a note of vulnerability in his tired tone.

"You have to understand."

"That's what I'm trying to do." Although Caine's voice remained calm, his eyes were not. "But you have to remember that I'm just a dumb jock. So perhaps you'd better try speaking slowly. And stick to words with no more than two syllables."

Caine's passion had always simmered just below the surface. Such intensity had always been exciting to Nora. At this moment, she was discovering that it could also be frightening.

Her nerves in a tangle, she pulled the rumpled sheet up to cover her breasts. "What we shared was wonderful, Caine. It always was. But it's not enough."

How could such an intelligent woman not see that after such intense lovemaking, she belonged to him? The same way he belonged to her.

"It's not enough because you won't let it be," he argued. "We both finally came home tonight, Nora. Where we belong. I want to spend all the rest of my nights with you, for fifty—hell, if we're lucky—even sixty or seventy-five years.

"I want to go to sleep every night with my arms wrapped around you and I want to wake up every morning knowing that you're beside me. I want to grow old with you, Nora."

Dear Lord, that's what she wanted, too. But there was something else. Something she knew he was leaving out.

"What about children?"

Don't let me mess this up, he begged whatever unforeseen fates had taken control of their lives.

Caine took a deep breath and chose his words very carefully.

"I know you've always considered me selfish. And perhaps I am. Because since coming back to Tribulation, I've discovered I want it all, sweetheart.

"I want to marry you and live in a house with a white picket fence. I want a stupid, friendly mutt who'll track mud in on the freshly washed floors, steal the steaks off the backyard barbecue and dig up the tulip bulbs every spring.

"And yes, I want children."

This was probably one of the longest speeches he'd ever made in his life. Reminding himself that it was also the most important, Caine took a deep breath.

"The best thing we ever did, in spite of ourselves, was create Dylan," he said, his voice gruff with emotion. "I love you, Nora. I want to have a family with you. Kids, Mom, Pop, a dog, the works."

Nora went ice-cold. Hands, feet, heart. "And where is this dream house going to be located? Detroit? And for how long?"

He flinched, knowing she had a point. There had been a time when he'd been so caught up in chasing his own dream, he would have thought nothing of dragging his family across the country, from town to town, wherever there was a baseball stadium.

"I didn't realize that the word had already gotten out."

"What word?"

"That I'd been offered the coaching job in Detroit."

"Oh." Amazingly, she hadn't known. Maggie's death had definitely put a crimp in Tribulation's rapid-fire gossip line. "Congratulations."

Caine shrugged. "I turned it down."

It was one more surprise in a night of surprises. "Why?"

Caine stared down at her in disbelief. Hadn't she been listening to a single word he'd said? "So I could stay in Tribulation. With you."

"I can't let you turn down an opportunity to stay in baseball for me."

"I'm not turning it down entirely because of you, Nora. I'd already decided to take over Maggie's charter business. It was what Gram wanted and the more I thought about it, the more I found myself liking the idea."

The decision had proven surprisingly easy. In the beginning, before Maggie's death, he'd suspected that the odds of Nora being willing to leave Tribulation and follow him to Detroit were slim to none. But, dammit, he'd told himself over and over again, he wasn't asking her to give up medicine; she could practice in Detroit. Perhaps, he'd considered, if he couched things carefully, he could make her understand that baseball had always been, aside from her and Dylan, the most important thing in his life.

But by the time he'd finished polishing the cabin windows he'd realized that he didn't really want to return to living out of a suitcase, never having any sense of belonging.

What he wanted was for him and Nora to sink their own family roots into the forest soil of a town that had been home to so many generations of Andersons and O'Hallorans.

"So you're staying?" She'd be seeing him almost every day. On the street, in the market, perhaps even here at the clinic. The idea was as terrifying as it was wonderful.

"For good."

"Well...if it's what you really want to do..."

"It is." Sighing, he linked their fingers together and brought them to his lips. "I told you, downstairs, that I was going to leave before I stooped to begging, but dammit, if that's what it takes—"

"No." She pressed the fingers of her free hand against his mouth, silencing him. "There's nothing you can say that'll change my mind, Caine."

"Nothing? Are you sure about that?"

"Positive."

Instead of moving away, as she had expected him to, Caine drew her close. He pressed his lips against her temple. "You're far too passionate a woman to give up what we have together." He kissed her eyelids. Her cheek. Her chin.

"You said I could always make you fly," he murmured, his lips gently brushing against her mouth. "But I only ever felt that way with you. Let's fly together, Nora. You and me. Forever."

His words and his kisses caused a renewed flare of warmth. Against all common sense, Nora tilted her head back, giving his mouth access to her throat.

A soft silvery mist was fogging her senses, her body began to yearn. "I want to," she told him in a shuddering whisper.

"I know." His mouth skimmed down her throat, along her collarbone. Caine tugged the sheet free. "So why not marry me?"

When his tongue stroked wetly along the aching slope of her breasts, Nora realized that she was teetering once again on the very edge of seduction.

"Because," she managed, "you want a family."

Caine was already imagining her hot and hungry beneath him. He was already remembering the soft little sounds she made when he made her rise, the look of astonished pleasure in her eyes when he took her over the edge. But Nora's unexpected words sliced through his erotic fantasy like a sharp knife.

"Are you telling me that you don't?" That idea had never occurred to him.

"No." Her skin, which had been warm and prettily flushed from their lovemaking, had turned as cold as ice and as pale as sleet. "I don't."

Moisture pooled in her distressed brown eyes.

Comprehension, when it dawned, was staggering.

"It's because of Dylan, isn't it?" A single tear escaped; Caine reached out and brushed it away. "Nora, sweetheart, what happened to Dylan was an accident. It could never happen again."

Didn't he think she knew that? She was an intelligent woman. She had a wall downstairs covered with degrees to prove it. But that didn't expunge the absolute fear she felt whenever she thought about having another baby.

Loving a child was the greatest treasure any woman could ever know. And the greatest peril. And although she'd never considered herself a coward, Nora didn't think she had the strength to ever face such risk again.

"I don't want to talk about Dylan." Her hands pushed ineffectually at his chest.

Caine tightened his hold. "Dammit, Nora. I can understand what you're feeling. I can understand why you're afraid. But although life doesn't come with guarantees, I love you and you love me and that should be enough to get us through any storms that might come along."

"I can't handle it, Caine," Nora insisted, her voice rising unnaturally high. "Losing Dylan almost destroyed me. I won't risk that pain again. Not even for you."

"Not even for us?"

"No." The tears were flowing freely now. Nora dashed at them with the backs of her hands. "Not even for us."

"All right."

Caine dropped his hands to his sides although he wanted to go on holding her. Nearly as quickly as he'd dispensed with them in the first place, he located his scattered clothes and dressed while Nora watched silently, not trusting his sudden acquiescence.

"I'm going to leave now," he said, after he'd finished buttoning his shirt. "But there's something you need to know."

"What now?"

"Loving someone doesn't necessarily mean losing them."

He bent down, captured her chin in his fingers and held her wary gaze to his. "This time, I'm not going to get in my car and drive away, just because things have gotten a little rough."

A little rough? Her heart was lying in tatters all over the floor and he was calling things a little rough?

"I love you, Nora Anderson O'Halloran," he said, feeling an ache deep inside when his words and his use of her married name made her flinch. "Fully, totally, irrevocably. With every fiber of my being.

"And being an admittedly greedy man, I intend to spend the rest of my life making love with you here in this bed, or in front of a roaring fire, or even in the lake behind my cabin."

"We'd drown," Nora couldn't resist saying.

He smiled at that and she knew she was in major trouble when the sight warmed her to the core. "Not if we're careful." He ran his finger down the slope of her nose. "How long can you hold your breath?"

Before she could respond, he gave her a quick, hard kiss. "What do you think about an August wedding? The weather should be warm and sunny and your grandmother's flowers will be in full bloom, so we can hold the ceremony in her garden."

He was doing it again—refusing to listen to a word she said. Nora welcomed the burst of irritation; it overrode her pain.

"Caine, we're not going to get married."

"Wanna bet? Or are you afraid to put your money where that luscious mouth of yours is?"

She'd never been able to resist that challenge in his eyes. "All right, dammit. Fifty dollars."

"That's chicken feed. Five hundred says you'll be Mrs. Nora O'Halloran before the summer's over."

It was more than she could safely risk. But frustration at the way some things never changed made Nora rash. "You're on."

"Terrific." He brushed a hand down her hair and followed the corn-silk strands around her jaw. "Remind me to remind you of this conversation on our fiftieth anniversary. When we're sitting on the porch in our rocking chairs, holding hands and watching our grandchildren splashing around in the lake behind the cabin."

"For the last time—"

He bent his head and touched his mouth to hers. "See you around, sweetheart," he said when the brief, possessive kiss ended. "Call me when you've changed your mind."

And then, to her astonishment, he was gone.

Nora sat there in the middle of the rumpled sheets still redolent of their lovemaking, and listened to Caine take the stairs two at a time.

Downstairs, the grandfather clock struck the hour with a flurry of Westminster chimes. She heard the front door open, then close. And then there was only silence.

Dark, lonely silence.

13

ALTHOUGH CAINE SPOKE with Nora on the phone almost daily, filling her in on the progress of the trauma center, he managed, with herculean effort, to keep his promise to stay away for four long and lonely weeks.

Despite the fact that the charter business was booming, he made time to talk public-relations firms in New York, Washington, D.C., and Seattle into donating their services. In addition, he'd convinced the governor to agree to declare the first week in September Children's Safety Week.

And if that wasn't enough to make his ex-wife sit up and take notice, an Academy Award-winning movie director Caine had once met at a New York premier was traveling around the country, filming a documentary about children in the emergency room. The Dylan Anderson O'Halloran Memorial Foundation was only paying the director's expenses; when contacted by Caine, the woman had agreed to donate her time and equipment.

Although Nora knew it took more than PR and governmental declarations and films to build a hospital, all the proclamations and public relations had already brought in a stunning amount of money.

As she watched Caine's unflagging devotion to this cause, which was so important not only to her, personally, but to all the children of the state, Nora was forced to admit how badly she'd misjudged him.

And with that realization came a long hard look at her own life. It wasn't that she'd purposely shied away from marriage since her divorce. In the beginning, work had required all her energy. Then, once she'd begun to date, she'd quickly discovered that although men might not be imbued with a woman's biological clock, they all definitely seemed to possess a strong sense of dynasty.

After Dylan's death, Nora had vowed never to give birth to another child. The risk was too great, the pain of loss too overwhelming. Whenever the man she was dating realized that she had no intention of bearing his child, he would drift on in quest of some woman who would, leaving Nora alone. Again.

The truth was, Nora was tired of being alone. The even greater truth was that there was only one man she wanted to share her life with. A month ago, Nora had been trying to convince herself that marrying Caine would be impossible. Now she knew that the impossibility would be *not* marrying him.

More nervous than she'd ever been in her life, and more determined, Nora left the hospital at the end of her shift and headed for the airstrip. Toward her future.

Caine had just landed a red-and-white six-seater Beech Bonanza aircraft and was taxiing to the hangar when he saw Nora's car headed down the road toward the tarmac.

"It's about time." He was on the ground, but his heart was suddenly back in the air.

"Handles like a dream, doesn't she?" the enthusiastic salesman beside him said, misunderstanding Caine's murmured statement. "And the club seating in the back is perfect for your kind of recreational charter work."

"She's a sweetheart, all right," Caine agreed, trying to keep his mind on bringing the turbocharged plane to a gradual stop when what he wanted to do was jump out of the cockpit, run across the tarmac, sweep Nora into his arms like some crazed guy in a shampoo commercial and never let her go again. She was parking next to his new blue Jeep Grand Cherokee.

"And the price is right," the man added.

"I said, I like the plane," Caine interrupted impatiently. He cut the engine, unfastened his seat belt and opened the pilot's door. "But something's come up. I've got your card. Why don't I call you tomorrow morning?"

Nora was getting out of her car. Caine saw a flash of thigh. "Make that tomorrow afternoon," he decided.

Business taken care of, he began briskly striding across the tarmac as Nora walked toward him.

They met halfway.

"Hi," she said softly.

"Hi, yourself."

"Nice plane. Is it new?"

"I'm thinking about buying it."

"Nice truck, too. Where's the Ferrari?"

He grinned. "I sold it. Figured it was time I bought a halfway grown-up car."

"It still suits you," Nora decided. Caine saw the flash of blue as she combed her left hand nervously through her hair. He caught her hand on its way down.

"I like your ring. It looks familiar."

"I like it, too." Breathless, Nora smiled up at him. "In fact, I was thinking about keeping it."

It was going to be all right, Caine realized. They were going to be all right. "Oh? For how long?"

"How does fifty or sixty years sound?"

"Not bad. For starters." He pulled her close and gave her a long, heartfelt kiss.

Nora threw her arms around his neck and kissed him back, earning a rousing cheer from the ground crew.

"Come on, sweetheart," Caine murmured huskily. "Let's get out of here. Before we have to start selling tickets."

"Which house?"

"For now, yours, because it's closer. But later, why don't we live in the cabin and save your place for your clinic?" he suggested. "Until we get you pregnant. Then we can build that house with the picket fence."

The minute he heard himself say the words, Caine realized he was pushing again. He held his breath, waiting for Nora to stiffen in his arms.

Surprisingly, the decision to have children, once Nora had accepted her feelings for Caine, hadn't proved as difficult as she'd feared. She had no doubt that Caine loved her. And she loved him.

And it was that love which made the risk worthwhile.

"That sounds like a wonderful solution," she agreed.

Relief came in cooling waves. With his arm wrapped around her waist, Caine began walking with her back to her car.

"By the way, Dr. Anderson, you owe me five hundred bucks."

She'd forgotten all about their ridiculous bet.

Happier than she could ever remember being, Nora threw back her head and laughed. "Luckily for me, I'm going to have a rich husband to pay off my gambling debts."

THE ROOM LOOKED AND smelled like an explosion at a Rose Bowl Parade. Flowers were everywhere; on the utilitarian pine dresser, the metal dining tray, the windowsill, the floor.

"Wow! Look at this!"

Eight-year-old Johnny O'Halloran, wearing a blue Little League uniform with O'Halloran Air Charters stenciled on the back in bright red letters, plucked a white card from an enormous white wicker basket overflowing with tiger lilies, creamy orchids, purple gladioli and trailing jasmine vines.

"Don Mattingly," he breathed with wonder.

"How soon they forget," Caine grumbled good-naturedly to Nora. "I can remember a time not all that long ago, when the kid had me up on that lofty pedestal."

"That was before you put him to work painting all those pickets," Nora reminded with an answering grin as she packed a box of fragrant dusting powder into her red overnight case.

Caine had surprised her with the scented powder while she'd been in labor. Using a soft, crystal-handled brush, with unerring accuracy he'd smoothed it over all her sensitive spots, making her forget, albeit for a short time, all about the pain.

"I didn't mind helping Dad out with the painting," Johnny said dismissively. "It was cleaning up those brushes and things that was such a drag."

"I remember feeling the same way when my dad put me to work scraping barnacles off the hull of *The Bountiful*," Caine said.

"That sounds a lot worse than cleaning paintbrushes," Johnny decided. "At least Eric helped."

"You boys were both a big help," Caine assured him. He refrained from bringing up the slight argument over territory that had ended with both boys looking like snowmen, covered head to foot in Glacier White ten-year-guaranteed outdoor latex.

"I know." Johnny roamed the room, scanning each card in turn, reading off the names that sounded like an All-

Star roster. "Gee, Cecil Fielder. Jose Canseco. Rickey Henderson."

He wove his way back through the colorful profusion of flowers and stood looking down at eight-pound, six-ounce Margaret Caitlin O'Halloran.

"You must be pretty special. To get all this stuff," he said to the baby, who looked up at him with bright blue eyes and made a soft cooing sound. "Even if you are a girl."

Sensing a possible sibling rivalry beginning to brew, Nora ran her hand down his arm. "You're special, too, Johnny."

"I know. Because you picked me out."

"That's right," Caine added, ruffling the blond hair that was only slightly darker than the fuzz atop his daughter's head.

Now that Johnny had put on some much-needed weight and his face had lost that worried, pinched expression, he looked like any other eight-year-old boy. He looked, Caine and Nora had agreed, as if he could have been their natural son.

"And you've no idea how glad we are that we did."

Last year, while flying to Hawaii for a honeymoon, Nora had tried to come up with some way to broach the idea of Johnny becoming part of their family. She needn't have worried. They'd no sooner arrived at their Kauai hotel when Caine suggested adopting the boy they'd both come to care for so deeply.

"I'm glad, too," Johnny said.

He reached out a finger and touched one of Caitlin's tiny pink hands; the baby closed a pudgy fist around his finger and held it with surprising strength. "And I guess I'm glad I've got a little sister. Even if I was kinda hoping for a boy."

"I didn't know that," Nora said.

"So I'd have someone to play ball with," Johnny explained. "Girls like dolls better than baseball."

"Don't say that too loudly around your mother," Caine suggested mildly, "or you'll have to listen to yet another lecture on women's equality."

"It sounds as if one is definitely in order," Nora told them. "But we'll save it for another day."

She glanced around the room, checking to see if she'd forgotten anything. "I think that's it." She frowned at the wheelchair beside the hospital bed. "I hate that thing."

"As a doctor, you should know it's hospital rules," Caine reminded. "Have a seat, sweetheart. Your chariot awaits."

After Nora reluctantly sat down in the chair, Caine took their daughter out of the bassinet and placed her in her mother's arms.

Feeling a surge of emotion so strong it rocked him, he brushed a quick kiss atop Caitlin's head, then kissed his wife, lingering for a moment over the sweet taste he knew he'd never tire of if he lived to be a hundred.

"Ugh. More mushy stuff," Johnny groaned.

"One of these days, you and I are going to have a long father-and-son talk," Caine said with a laugh. "About girls and kissing and all that other mushy stuff."

"I'd rather talk about batting averages," Johnny replied. "Besides, I already know where babies come from. We're learning about sex in school."

"They teach sex in school these days?" Caine asked in mock surprise. "What ever happened to spelling and long division?"

"They still have all that boring old stuff, too," Johnny informed him with a definite lack of enthusiasm. "And you and Mom both signed the permission slip, remember?"

"Now that you mention it, I do," Caine replied. "And to think my favorite class used to be recess," he murmured, earning a quick appreciative grin from Nora.

Putting his arm around his son's shoulder, Caine said, "Come on, gang, let's go home."

Nora smiled up at her husband of ten months. "Yes," she agreed. Her heart was shining in her eyes. "Let's all go home."

Home. As he walked out of the hospital into the bright sunshine with his family, Caine decided there was no more wonderful word in the entire English language.

American HEROES
AGAINST ALL ODDS

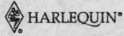 HARLEQUIN®

 Silhouette®

Please address questions and book requests to: Harlequin Reader Service U.S.: 3010 Walden Ave.,
P.O. Box 1325, Buffalo, NY 14269 CAN.: P.O. Box 609, Fort Erie, Ont. L2A 5X3   PAHGEN

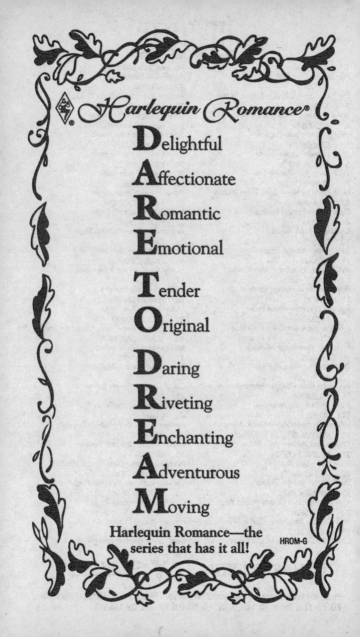

Harlequin Romance®

Delightful

Affectionate

Romantic

Emotional

Tender

Original

Daring

Riveting

Enchanting

Adventurous

Moving

Harlequin Romance—the
series that has it all!

HROM-G

HARLEQUIN PRESENTS®

The world's bestselling romance series...
The series that brings you your favorite authors,
month after month:

Helen Bianchin...Emma Darcy
Lynne Graham...Penny Jordan
Miranda Lee...Sandra Morton
Anne Mather...Carole Mortimer
Susan Napier...Michelle Reid

and many more uniquely talented authors!

Wealthy, powerful, gorgeous men...
Women who have feelings just like your own...
The stories you love, set in exotic, glamorous locations...

HARLEQUIN PRESENTS,
Seduction and passion guaranteed!

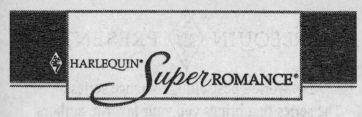

HARLEQUIN *Super*ROMANCE®

...there's more to the story!

Superromance.
A *big* satisfying read about unforgettable
characters. Each month we offer *six* very different
stories that range from family drama to adventure
and mystery, from highly emotional stories to
romantic comedies—and much more! Stories
about people you'llbelieve in and care about.
Stories too compelling to put down....

Our authors are among today's *best* romance
writers. You'll find familiar names and talented
newcomers. Many of them are award winners—
and you'll see why!

**If you want the biggest and best
in romance fiction, you'll get it
from Superromance!**

Available wherever Harlequin books are sold.

Visit us at www.eHarlequin.com

HSGEN00

HARLEQUIN®
Makes any time special.™

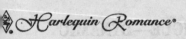

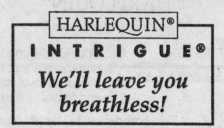